Last First Kiss

Special Edition

Montgomery Ink Legacy

Carrie Ann Ryan

Last First Kiss

Montgomery Ink Legacy NOVEL

By
Carrie Ann Ryan

LAST FIRST KISS

A Montgomery Ink Legacy Novel

By: Carrie Ann Ryan

Cover Art by Sweet N Spicy Designs

Photo by Wander Aguiar Photography

Praise for Carrie Ann Ryan

"Count on Carrie Ann Ryan for emotional, sexy, character driven stories that capture your heart!" – Carly Phillips, NY Times bestselling author

"Carrie Ann Ryan's romances are my newest addiction! The emotion in her books captures me from the very beginning. The hope and healing hold me close until the end. These love stories will simply sweep you away." - NYT Bestselling Author Deveny Perry

"Carrie Ann Ryan writes the perfect balance of sweet and heat ensuring every story feeds the soul." - Audrey Carlan, #1 New York Times Bestselling Author

"Carrie Ann Ryan never fails to draw readers in with passion, raw sensuality, and characters that pop off the page. Any book by Carrie Ann is an absolute treat." – New York Times Bestselling Author J. Kenner

"Carrie Ann Ryan knows how to pull your heartstrings and make your pulse pound! Her wonderful Redwood Pack series will draw you in and keep you reading long into the night. I can't wait to see what comes next with the new generation, the Talons. Keep them coming, Carrie Ann!" –Lara Adrian, New York Times bestselling author of CRAVE THE NIGHT

"With snarky humor, sizzling love scenes, and brilliant, imaginative worldbuilding, The Dante's Circle series reads as if Carrie Ann Ryan peeked at my personal wish list!" – NYT Bestselling Author, Larissa Ione

"Carrie Ann Ryan writes sexy shifters in a world full of passionate happily-ever-afters." – *New York Times* Bestselling Author Vivian Arend

“Carrie Ann’s books are sexy with characters you can’t help but love from page one. They are heat and heart blended to perfection.” *New York Times* Bestselling Author Jayne Rylon

Carrie Ann Ryan's books are wickedly funny and deliciously hot, with plenty of twists to keep you guessing. They'll keep you up all night!” USA Today Bestselling Author Cari Quinn

"Once again, Carrie Ann Ryan knocks the Dante's Circle series out of the park. The queen of hot, sexy, enthralling paranormal romance, Carrie Ann is an author not to miss!" *New York Times* bestselling Author Marie Harte

LAST FIRST KISS

The Montgomery Ink Legacy series continues with a workplace fling romance that starts off with a literal bang. Daisy Montgomery Knight is about to meet her match when it comes to Hugh Hendrix.

One look across the aisle at a wedding and I fell in lust.

He's on the bride's side. I'm on the groom's.

But by the end of the night, we're against a wall, over a table...and in bed.

I'm prepared never to see him again except in my memories.

Only the next week things become awkward: I'm his new boss.

And it turns out he's just as demanding outside of the sheets as beneath them.

We need to stay away from each other—he has his demons, as well as an adorable little girl, and I'm trying to heal after a job gone wrong.

I know I need to walk away...even if neither one of us wants to.

To Team Carrie Ann,

Thank you for being at my back and always being there for me.
You're the reason I get to do this.
And the reason I sometimes get to sleep.

Chapter One

Hugh

I wanted nothing more than to take off this ridiculous tie, slide off the shoes that were pinching my toes for some unknown reason, and find an ice-cold pint. I had so many other things on my plate, coming to this wedding hadn't been a huge priority. However, as the bride was a family friend, and I was the only one of my family currently living in America, somebody had to represent the family interests.

I could actually hear my mother's voice echo through my head as she said those exact words to me the week prior, ordering me to come.

I already bought the damn gift for Rina and Henry's wedding. It was from their registry, and I actually liked Rina. I'd never met Henry before, but Rina was a good friend when we were kids living in London. Now somehow both of us were living in Denver, Colorado, in America of all places. However, life had a way of derailing your plans and throwing you into a life that you never thought possible.

Before I was forced to move here, I thought Colorado was full of snow. Maybe some nice temperate weather days, but I was wrong. Apparently one could go through all the seasons in one day. It was a little chilly that morning and felt nice on my skin. Had reminded me of home. Both homes, where I lived for most of my life: New York and London. New York got hot of course, but the sun never felt like this. Maybe it was because we were so damn close to it at this elevation.

I didn't hate living here but it was still new, and I didn't have a sense of stability that I needed for me to be comfortable. As it was, I was spending my one free Saturday at the wedding of a woman I hadn't seen in near to a decade, just to please my family.

I hadn't done enough of that in the past, so I supposed I should probably remember why I said yes to this thing in the first place.

I was just so tired of changes.

"Hey, groom side or bride side?" a man with flaming

red hair and a bright grin asked. He had on the gray tuxedo the wedding party wore, along with the candy-pink accessories that did horrible things with his hair. I'm sure the pink-and-gray coloring worked with nearly everyone else, but as a fellow ginger, I sympathized with him that no one thought about what a redhead would look like in the wedding colors. Not that it mattered. This was Rina's day, and probably her husband's as well.

"Bride's," I finally answered.

"Okay cool, I'll go show you where you need to sit. How long have you known Rina?" the man asked, and I followed him to the seating area. I didn't need an usher to tell me where to sit, but if this was his job, and he was enjoying it, I wasn't going to stop him. I hadn't brought a date to the wedding, and I didn't know anyone here. That felt like that was going to be my lot in life for many things, because I didn't know anyone anywhere. Except the reason I moved here in the first place.

"We knew each other as kids. Our families are close."

The man grinned.

"I figured with the British accent you were on the bride's side, but I didn't want to assume, you know? Anyway, that's really cool that you flew all the way out here just to see her. I mean, just because you were friends as kids, it doesn't mean that you have to be friends now, you know?"

The guy was doing a good job of putting me at ease,

even though I was still tired from unpacking boxes most of the day yesterday.

"I'm sure Henry knows a few British people. Considering he's marrying one."

"That is true."

I went down the row he gestured to, one in the middle, not in the back where I wanted to be so I could hide and not have to deal with small talk. But at least I wasn't up in the front, although I would have to make eye contact with all of Rina's family and anyone passing by. I'd be able to blend in here better, so I appreciated this guy picking up on that.

"Anyway, welcome. And seriously, on behalf of the bride and groom, thanks for flying all the way out here for the wedding."

I shook my head. "I moved to Colorado, so it wasn't too far of a drive for me. Not across the pond," I said with the roll of my eyes because I hated the phrase.

"That's amazing. Small worlds and all that. I'm Josh by the way." He held out his hand and I shook it. I liked this guy, even though I would probably never see him again after today.

"Nice to meet you, Josh, I'm Hugh."

"Welcome to my favorite state in the world. Glorious sun, great places to ski, and the best food out there."

I raised a brow. "Are you sure about the food?"

"Aren't you from a place that doesn't use seasoning?" Josh asked, teasing.

I rolled my eyes. "Excuse me, but I take umbrage at that."

"Oh, do you?" Josh said with a laugh before someone called his name and he waved back.

"I better get back to work, but nice to meet you, Hugh." And then Josh was off, practically skipping towards couples waiting to be shown to their seats.

I rolled my eyes and took my seat, feeling slightly more energetic. Maybe today wouldn't be all that bad.

And then a little kid sneezed behind me, mucus landing on my neck.

I shuddered as the woman behind me apologized. I stood up and smiled, nodded as if I wasn't about to freak the fuck out over the amount of snot on me, and made my way to the restroom to hopefully wash my neck off before the wedding started.

I loved my daughter. Lucy was energetic, adorable, and I had dealt with enough bodily fluids that I could handle most things. But a stranger's kid? No thanks. I was already hot and sweaty, I didn't need to add anything else to make me more uncomfortable.

I turned the corner and bumped into a woman in sky-high heels, yet was still quite a bit shorter than me. I cursed and reached out, gripping her shoulders. She had her hand on my wrist in a moment, squeezing with a twist that surprised me. I knew that move. And if I wasn't careful, she was going to twist my arm around my back. Interesting.

Why did that make me hard? There was something wrong with me, and I needed to either get laid, or get some sleep. Probably both.

"I'm sorry. I wasn't watching where I was going, and I'm trying to be quick about it. I apologize." I gently moved my arms from her shoulders and tried not to stand agog with my mouth open. She was quite possibly the most gorgeous woman I had ever met in my life.

And, in my line of work, I tended to meet a lot of beautiful women.

She had stunning green eyes that looked as if they were crafted within the ocean. In fact, I bet in sunlight they looked gray or even blue. The mystery of it compelled me, and that probably should have been a warning sign. Her long dark hair was neatly crafted into some form of updo thing that I didn't understand. I wondered what it would look like if I pulled it out of its style, just to see it fall down her back. Would it be wavy? Would it easily wrap around my fist?

She was strong, muscular, a little above average height, but still short next to me.

She had curves, beautiful breasts that filled out her

dress achingly well, and slightly widened hips, the perfect width for my grip.

I shook myself out of whatever the hell was going on with me. I did not react to women like this. Hell, I barely reacted at all these days. I was too busy trying to keep up with my daughter, this move, and the fact that I would start a new job on Monday. I didn't have time for this wedding.

"It's okay," the woman said, her voice slightly smoky. It was a voice that drew me.

What the hell was wrong with me?

"Anyway, I should hurry. Don't want to be late."

Her red tinted lips quirked into a smile, and I swallowed hard.

"No, I don't think Henry's bride will appreciate that."

"You're on the groom side then?"

She nodded. "And with that accent, I guess you're on the bride's side?"

"You know, you're not the first person to say that today. Your friend could know more than one British person, not just the one he's marrying."

"True. But statistically, I think Rina knows a few more."

"You know, you're probably right."

"Anyway, I will see you. At least across the aisle." She

winked, before she turned towards the wedding center, her hips swaying just right. I didn't think she was doing it on purpose either. It was those damn heels, and those legs that went on for days. And she was so damn strong. So muscular.

I shook that off, because I didn't want to walk into the wedding after it started, and ran to the bathroom, cleaned the back of my neck, washed my hands, and let out a breath as I leaned on the sink.

"You can do this. One more day of being normal."

Whatever normal was.

I made it to my seat in the middle pew right as the processions began. I was grateful that I hadn't had to slip in the middle of it or hide behind a pillar during the damn ceremony. That would've been just my luck.

Of course, it seemed my luck was changing, because as I turned to watch the procession, I saw the dark-haired beauty right across from me. She winked as the man next to her spoke into her ear and she laughed, a nice husky laugh that went straight to my groin.

She had brought a fucking date. I guess that answered that.

Now to just get my cock to agree.

Soon Rina was walking down the aisle, and I did my best to pay attention to my childhood friend and not the woman who seemed to ignite something that had been dormant for a very long time.

The wedding went off without a hitch and the bride and groom seemed perfect for each other. Not that I actually believed that. Perfection was an illusion, and marriages didn't last. I was testament to that, as were most of my friends. If I was a more cynical man, I would take bets on how long this would last. After all, Rina and Henry came from different places, had known each other less than a year, and yet they were promising a life together. I wasn't sure that was going to work, but maybe they would have fun along the way. I hoped it would be better than mine.

I made my way to the reception and got an old fashioned. I sipped the drink, letting the walnut bitters settle over my tongue.

One hour closer to taking off this damned tie.

I checked in with the babysitter and was told Lucy was doing great. I smiled at the photo on my phone of Lucy beaming up at me, her bright red hair in curls all around her face.

She looked a lot like my family, not so much her mother's. I wouldn't say that was a bad thing, but I would never tell that to my child. She still loved her mother, despite everything that woman had done.

"Your face went from relaxed to smiling to angry. Now I have to know what you're looking at."

I smiled as I slid my phone into my pocket and looked up at the woman with dark hair.

"Just family things," I said smoothly. Lucy was mine. I didn't like bringing her up to strangers, not when people would want to know why I was a single father. That wasn't information I wanted blasted about.

"Well, family does that," the woman said, a smile playing on her face as if she had a secret joke. "Anyway, I'm Daisy."

I smiled. "Hugh." I looked over her shoulder. "Where's your date?" I asked, only a little annoyed with myself for caring, but really fucking annoyed with myself for the tone. Her eyebrow shot up as she frowned before she snapped her fingers. "No. Not my date. That would be Crew. He's my best friend, and one of the biggest pains in my ass. He's out searching for a bridesmaid that winked at him during the ceremony. I don't have the heart to tell him that she's a lesbian and I think she was winking at me."

I burst out laughing and shook my head.

"Well, then I'm Hugh. Though I feel like I already did this."

She tipped her champagne glass to my lowball glass and smiled. "It's nice to meet you, Hugh. So, are you ready to relax a bit? Weddings always stress me out."

"Been to a lot of weddings, have you?"

That made her laugh, and I wondered what the story was there. "You have no idea, and I have a few more coming up."

"But not yours."

"So subtle," she said with a laugh.

"I'm really rusty at this."

"Honestly, same. But this is fun. And no, not mine. I'm single."

"Same."

Her eyes filled with warmth, and when her tongue darted out to lick her lips, I swallowed hard.

"Good to know."

"Yes, very good."

Tonight might be more interesting than I thought.

"Okay, time to catch the garter," the announcer said over the mic.

I groaned. "I hate this."

"Go, make your friend happy."

"I really don't believe Rina's going to care if I have a garter that she wore thrown at my face. If anything, she'll probably kick my ass."

"She'll kick your ass if you break tradition. Now go," she said, taking my drink.

"I wasn't done with that."

"You can come back and get it later. I'll hold it hostage for now."

I rolled my eyes and made my way out with the other single men, letting the ringbearer and all his friends stand in front of me. If I was lucky, I'd toss a child at the garter or one of the guys next to me and run.

Marriage wasn't for me, and I had no plans on ever doing it again. I realized when people said that out loud, it usually jinxed them, but not me. I had already been married once. It ended in such a spectacular failure that my life had changed twice. I wasn't fucking doing it again.

"Oh hey, you're here," Josh said as he came to my side with a grin on his face.

"Hello there."

"You ready to tackle someone for the garter?"

"I can push you towards it," I said dryly.

"That sounds like a challenge."

I opened my mouth to say something, but lace slapped me in the face.

I instinctively reached out, then looked down at the damn garter in my hand.

Josh pulled out his phone and snapped a photo while grinning.

See. Tempting fate.

"Please take it," I said, trying to toss the thing at him.

Josh held up both hands.

"Don't break tradition."

"Oh, it's you!" Rina said as she ran towards me, the train of her dress in hand. "That's not awkward at all," she said as she went to her tiptoes and kissed me on the cheek.

I rolled my eyes because it was hard to be angry at Rina for anything, let alone this.

"I'm going to get you back for this."

"You tossed me into a mud pit when we were three, I think this is payback."

"You're the one who tossed me first," I countered.

"So this is the infamous Hugh," Henry said as he held out his hand. I shook it. The groom beamed, looking so in love with his wife, I wanted to believe this could work for them.

"It's nice to meet you," I said.

"Likewise. Seriously, I could have been jealous of the way that Rina talks about you, but I realized that you're like the pesky brother."

That made me roll my eyes, relaxing a bit. "Maybe. But she's the pesky sister."

"And you love it," Rina said with a laugh as she sank into her husband's side. "And now it's time to toss the bouquet. Okay, Hugh, out of the way," she said with a laugh. I moved to the side and plucked both drinks from Daisy's hands. She looked nearly on the edge of tears from laughter. I chugged my drink and set the empty glass aside.

"Okay, it's your turn."

"Oh, I don't think so."

I practically pushed her towards the other women. "Payback's a bitch," I whispered.

A waiter handed me another glass of champagne but I held hers safe. I was only a little bit surprised when Daisy ducked out of the way, yet still ended up with the bouquet.

She glared at me before stomping over, ignoring the congratulations of others.

I shook my head when she took her drink back and chugged it.

Then she took my drink, tossed it back quickly, and set both glasses down on the tray next to her.

"I blame you for this."

I held up the garter.

"Oh, I blame you."

When people started shouting for us to dance, I shook my head, but she sighed.

"Let's get this over with."

"Really? You sound like dancing with me is going to be a problem."

She looked over her shoulder, her hand in mine, and I nearly tripped.

"Oh, this is going to be fun. But I don't make any promises."

I pulled her into my arms, dancing to whatever music filled the air. I leaned down and brushed my lips against hers. Just a brief kiss, but she nearly tripped.

People cheered, but I ignored them.

"Oh, I think this could be fun."

"Promises, promises," she mumbled as we continued to dance.

I had a feeling that tonight was only just beginning.

Chapter Two

Daisy

I knew I was being hit on. And I was hitting right back. I was perfectly fine with what was happening, because this was fun. I didn't get to have fun these days, according to my family members and coworkers. They enjoyed explaining to me that I needed more of a life than just work, girl time, and staying at home alone with my cheeseboard and glass of wine. Apparently, that wasn't a life.

Hugh slid his hand over my hip, slightly lower than I normally would've allowed, as we danced around the ballroom. I'm sure someone said something to me, something about congratulating me for being the next in line for a wedding because I caught the bouquet, but I ignored them.

"Why do I feel like your attention isn't on me, but on whatever is going on in that head of yours?" Hugh murmured.

There was just something about that accent of his. Give me a man with a British accent and I swooned. Thanks to Orlando Bloom showing up on screen with his long blond hair, staring off into the distance with those elf eyes of his. Then of course there was Henry Cavill, and every other British heartthrob.

It was definitely a problem.

I had to remind myself that we were in public, and while this was fun, and he sure knew how to dance, we were just two people enjoying themselves.

"Again, you're not paying attention to me." He squeezed my hip then took my hand and twirled me. I laughed, grateful for the dancing lessons I took when I was younger. My mom had wanted to learn how to two-step and waltz beyond just following Dad's lead, so she and I went on a mother-daughter dance trip. It had been a blast, and really cemented us as mom and kid rather than stepmom and kid.

My mother had always been in my life, even when she was just my dad's friend. I used to call her Aunt Adrienne.

When my birth mother decided it was easier to be a full-time businesswoman in another country rather than a mom, and that having a kid would dampen her lifestyle, I had gone to live with my dad. And Adrienne had been there. Just as his friend at first, at least that's what they told me. I had been too young to notice anything more. All I knew was that my dad and Adrienne loved each other and loved me. I had been one happy kid.

I hadn't even had time to truly grieve what my mother had done to me. Because Adrienne had always been there. My mom had always been there.

So I was grateful for those dance lessons for many reasons.

"You know how to dance. Do they teach that in every private boarding school in London?" I teased.

"You're just going to throw a stereotype at me?" he asked as he led me around the dance floor.

"Perhaps. Did you go to a boarding school?"

He rolled his eyes. "Only for high school. I'll have you know I was in other schools before that."

I threw my head back and laughed, while he just winked at me.

"I guess you're living the stereotype."

"Perhaps. But if I had gone to an all-boys boarding school when I was younger, I wouldn't have met Rina, and I wouldn't have been invited to this wedding."

"So, I have to be thankful that you met her on what, the playground?"

"Well, I wasn't going to push her in a mud puddle outside of that," he mumbled.

I grinned. "So, you and Rina never..." I let my voice trail off, and he choked.

"No. Not even a little. She had a crush on my best friend, and they dated for a little while, until they realized they were not good for each other, and we all just ended up being friends."

"And now you've moved here. To America."

"That's a long story," he said carefully, his gaze meeting mine.

I understood. Tonight wasn't about long stories. No, tonight was something a little more fun.

"So, how long have you known Henry?" he asked, and I heard the question in that.

"Since college. And no, we never dated. I think I was just invited because he wanted to make sure he had a comparable amount of people on his side of the aisle as hers."

That made him laugh, and damn it, he looked really good when he laughed.

This might be a problem. Or not. It wasn't like I was ever going to see this guy again. So we could have fun. Just for the evening.

My thoughts must have shown on my face because

his gaze darkened, going that smoky gray that made me want to press my thighs together. And that was quite a feat, considering we were dancing in public.

"So, you didn't come here with anyone?"

I shook my head. "Just Crew. My friend," I added quickly.

"Good."

And he somehow danced me off the dance floor.

"How about a drink?" he asked as we stepped off the dance floor, the song changing to something a little more fast-paced.

I slid my arm into his as he led me towards the bar.

"A drink would be nice. Although I've already had a lot of champagne."

He raised a brow. "So a sparkling cider or water then? Don't want you to drive home on too much alcohol. Or any for that matter."

I shook my head quickly. "No, I actually have a room here."

He raised that brow again, that stinking sexy brow. I was normally a forearm girl, but here I was, having tingly feelings thanks to an eyebrow.

"I thought you were local."

"I am. But I was here yesterday helping Rina and Henry with a few things because of my job."

"Should I ask what your job is? Are you a wedding planner?"

For some reason I didn't want him to know. Because most guys got weird about it. They didn't like a woman with such a traditionally male-centered job. I never understood it, but they always got weird and wanted to prove that they were stronger than me. They wanted to prove that I only got the job because of my family, not for my own strength and skills.

I just shook my head, and he nodded as if he understood.

"I'm not a wedding planner, if that helps," I added, then I winked and took the glass of champagne he offered. He clinked his glass to mine without taking his gaze from mine. I drank a little deeper than I usually would, my throat suddenly parched.

And without another word, I turned, because I had made this decision before that drink.

Tonight would be fun. I wasn't going to be lost in my own memories. Lost in my own woes.

I ignored the pain in my leg, the one that started at my hip and went down my knee all the way to my ankle. That wouldn't bother me tonight.

We made our way to the elevator, still sipping our champagne, gazes meeting without saying a word. He wanted this too. He wouldn't be following me to my hotel room if he didn't.

My glass was empty when we made it to my floor, and I quickly put the key against the door and let myself in. I set the glass on the table, and continued into the room, knowing my hips swayed side to side and feeling his gaze on them.

Good.

This was fun.

I never got to feel sexy, desired. I was too busy working, and going through PT. Now, though, now I could just be.

I heard his glass hit the counter, but then he was on me, and I hadn't realized he'd moved.

He took my hips and moved me so my hands were on the wall, my breath coming in pants.

"First names only?" he whispered.

"Nothing more."

"Oh, I think I can give you a bit more," he replied, his breath against my neck, and then his mouth was on my skin and I was arching into him. My ass pressed against his groin, and I could feel the hard length of him.

I swallowed hard, licking my lips.

Damn, this man was trouble. But the best kind of trouble.

There would be no promises, no tomorrows, and I was thankful for that.

I just wanted to have fun.

And from the way his hand slowly slid up my leg and up my dress, so did he.

"Is this what you want?" he asked, and I nodded against the wall.

"No, I'm going to need the words. I can't see your face, and I don't know your eyes yet. So tell me—what do you want?"

If I could come by the man ensuring consent, I would have. Perhaps it was just the accent, perhaps it was him making sure he wasn't reading the situation wrong. After all, I had been the one to invite him to my room, but I hadn't said anything. I just led him with my hips.

But I wanted this.

Even if it was only for an evening.

"Please. You and me. Just one night. Nothing but first names, and really hot orgasms." I turned in his arms so I could meet his gaze, and he was so close to me, my breasts pressed against his chest.

"I think I can do that," he growled, and then his lips were on mine, and I was falling. I slid my hands up and down his back, my fingernails digging in as he deepened the kiss, his tongue exploring my mouth. He tasted of champagne and a little bit of whiskey, and I craved him.

Somehow his hand was underneath my skirt, pulling my thong to the side, and then his fingers were diving between my legs. I groaned, my head falling back to the wall as he licked and bit my neck, his fingers exploring me. When he slid one finger into me, then a second, I groaned, arching over his hand.

"So fucking wet. Just one touch and you're already wet for me."

"Just get me off. Please," I begged, and he grinned.

"I think I can do that."

I slid my hand between us, covering his length over his pants. "And then you?"

"Then me," he promised, and he crushed his mouth to mine, sliding a third finger deep inside. I didn't know how he did it, with his thumb over my clit, but he fucked me with his fingers. I came, my body tensing, my pussy clamping around him. It was so quick, my nipples hardening under his attention, I could barely think. But I was moaning into his mouth, trying not to fall on my knees. He kept his hand on my hip, which was the only thing keeping me upright. And when I finally came down from my oblivion, he was still touching me.

Still deep inside me.

He slid his fingers out of me, and I groaned at the loss, before he took his other hand, pinched my chin so I'd meet his gaze, and then he licked one finger, then a second, and I groaned at the sight, my knees going weak. Then he took his third finger and slid it over my mouth.

"Suck," he ordered.

I opened my mouth, and I could taste myself on his

fingers. It was so damn erotic, so sensual, and something I'd never done before.

I liked sex. But I was usually quite quick at it, not like this.

This was something different.

And I wanted more.

When he was finished, he gripped my hips and picked me up. I wrapped my arms around his waist and he carried me to the bed.

When he set me down, he stripped my dress off me, unzipping the back, and I stepped out of it, standing in just my thong, bra, and heels.

"So beautiful," he groaned, and then he was kissing me, his hands on my breasts, down my hips, between my thighs.

He undid my bra, my breasts falling into his hands, and he sucked on them, biting and licking. Each tug went straight to my pussy, and I started pulling at his tie and jacket.

"I need you naked."

"We can make that happen."

He stood back as I toed off my shoes, my leg starting to hurt but I didn't want him to see. I didn't want reality disrupting the moment, so I ignored it and my pain.

I watched as he undid his tie, slid off his jacket, and undid one button after another.

He was going far too slow, so I pulled at his shirt,

unbuttoning it quickly. He laughed and I joined him, until he was shirtless and I nearly swallowed my tongue.

"You must like to work out."

"I could tell you why, but that would be too many details," he said and winked as I slid my hands down the hard ridges of his abdomen.

He was all strength, and ink, and that did something to me.

I liked ink, I liked muscles, and I liked men.

And damn it, he was way too sexy for his own good.

I helped him undo his belt, and then quickly undid his pants. Before he could say anything, I was pulling him out of his boxer briefs, groaning at the thick feel of him in my hand. He was long and wide and I could barely touch my fingertips around the girth of him.

"Oh my," I teased, and he winked at me.

"Please keep going," he said with a laugh, and I licked my lips before I slowly lowered my head.

His hands slid through my hair, guiding me. I swallowed him down, cupping his balls in my hands as I went down on him, hollowing my cheeks. When the tip of his dick pressed the back of my throat and I realized he still had more to go, I grinned, humming along his length.

"Daisy, hell," he muttered, that British accent getting rougher.

I continued to move, bobbing my head as I used my free hand to circle the length of him.

When he tensed, and I licked the tip of his dick, he pulled at my hair, pulling me back.

"No, I need to be inside you."

And then he was shoving off his pants and shoes, and I was wiggling out of my panties.

"Shit, condom. No mistakes."

He nodded. "I've got one."

I raised a brow and he scowled.

"You're really going to complain about that right now? That I always have one on me just in case?"

"I have one in my purse too. I like that we're both thinking ahead."

"Damn straight," he growled, before he kissed me hard again, and reached for his condom.

"I guess that means we could go for a round two. Just saying. If you're good enough."

He snorted. "I think I can make that happen."

And then he was sliding the condom over his length.

What was it about that action that was so fucking hot?

He was suddenly above me, gripping both thighs. I groaned when he pushed my knees to my earlobes and slammed right inside me. No hesitation, no waiting, just fullness.

I shouted his name, and then he was kissing me.

It was rough and fast and hot and needy, and I scraped my fingernails down his back, needing more.

When he rolled me to my stomach in one quick motion and I didn't even know it was happening, I groaned, letting him spread me wide as he slammed back into me. I went up to my hands and knees, meeting him thrust for thrust, while he used one hand to grip my hip, the other to play with my breasts.

"Hugh," I panted.

"That's it, Daisy. Keep working for me."

And then I pushed him back and laughed before we were rolling again, and I was sliding on top of him, needing him. The ache without him was too much.

I slid down over him, my hands on his shoulders to keep steady, meeting his gaze, seeing the parting of his lips, and I knew this could be trouble.

But thankfully it was only one night.

When I came, clamping around him, he followed closely, his hands on my breasts.

Just one night, I reminded myself.

And later, when we had each other one more time, after eating french fries and overcooked steaks, I let him take me in the shower, and over the counter, knowing I was going to be sore tomorrow for many reasons.

But it didn't matter. I fell asleep in his arms, exhausted, knowing that I would miss this, but at least I enjoyed myself.

When I woke up and he wasn't there, with no

number, no note, just the scent of him on the sheets, I smiled and told myself I didn't regret it. I couldn't.

Even if I wanted to know who he was, it was just one night. Just one set of fun.

We had done what we wanted to accomplish.

And I couldn't have regrets.

I just had reality.

And all the pains and aches that came with it.

Chapter Three

Daisy

"I cannot believe how big you're getting," I said with a laugh as my cousin flipped me off. "So ladylike."

Lake narrowed her gaze, her hand resting on the swell of her belly. "I'll have you know that this baby and I are going to kick your ass if you call me big one more time. I'm delicate. Sweet. Innocent. And not a cow."

I snorted and reached over to steal a piece of her toast. She slapped my fingers, and I grinned.

"How dare you steal from a pregnant woman."

"Well, I was going to try to steal from a pregnant

cow," I teased, and she tossed a cherry tomato at me. I caught it, glad we were at a friend's restaurant in downtown Denver, rather than someplace we could get kicked out.

"I see your aim is getting better," I teased.

"I have always been better than you at softball, thank you. And Nick is teaching me."

I rolled my eyes at the mention of her husband and my friend. "As if he doesn't know your softball skills." I popped the cherry tomato in my mouth and sighed happily.

We were at Taboo, a restaurant downtown owned by a family friend. It happened to be connected to the restaurant, the café, and coffee shop owned by our friends that was also attached to the tattoo shop and my security place. We were all in the family, and I loved it. While most of the time we ate at Latte on the Rocks, considering it was right next door to Montgomery Ink Too and Montgomery Security, Lake had an appointment downtown at her main job, doing her best to own the world, so I had come down here to meet her for breakfast. It helped that I could see some of my cousins, aunts, and uncles, as well as family friends that I didn't get to see on a daily basis.

"I still can't believe you just called me a cow."

"I didn't. I was commenting on the fact that you called yourself a cow."

"No, I said nobody's allowed to call me a cow. There's a difference."

I nodded sagely. "You're right. And you like being big because that means you're getting closer to baby."

A soft smile spread over her face, one that seemed to brighten up the whole room. "It doesn't seem real. It feels like just yesterday Nick and I were fighting like cats and dogs, and falling in hate with each other."

"That was yesterday. You guys use fighting as foreplay."

"Okay, that's true, but you're not supposed to comment on it," she said with a laugh.

"Anyway, how is baby doing? And soon-to-be Daddy?"

"We're all doing fine," Lake said as she rubbed her stomach. "You're coming to the baby shower, right? I know we said it could be co-ed, but Nick wants nothing to do with baby games or frilly dresses."

"Such a guy," I said with a roll of my eyes. "Though I could do without the whole guess what baby food is in the diaper game."

Lake shuddered and set down her fork. "I was just about to eat. Thank you for that memory."

"Well, don't worry, I know that Brooke won't let you down. She's been through the baby shower scene before."

Lake smiled at the thought of our cousin-in-law,

Brooke Montgomery, mother of two, and the most kick-ass woman that I knew.

"I admire her, the fact that she did this on her own the first time."

I nodded, remembering Brooke had lost the father of her first child in a tragic accident before the baby was born. She had been a single mother until she reconnected with our cousin Leif, and that was the end of that. Love at second sight, perhaps even at first and third, and then marriage, and a new baby. Everybody was moving on, finding happiness, getting married, getting engaged, and having babies. Not all of my cousins were on that path. In fact, most weren't, but they were getting closer. Hell, even our friends were getting married and thinking about having children.

I had always thought perhaps it could be my path. Perhaps if I got as lucky as my friends and family, I would find someone for me. I just wasn't sure that was in the cards for me. It wasn't like I was reaching old age without finding a guy who flipped my switch, but I hadn't found anything more than pleasant nights, or relationships that turned into some of my favorite friendships.

I wasn't going to think about the man the weekend before, the heat and the connection. I didn't even know his last name. I knew nothing about him other than what he felt like inside me, or the way that his accent got deeper when he was coming.

No, I wouldn't think about that.

Nor would I think about the fact that every wedding I had coming up was for a friend or family member, and I would be bringing Crew as my date. Because I wasn't about to go alone, but I still would have to deal with the questions about why I was bringing a friend. And why that friend happened to be my ex-boyfriend.

Crew and I got along, and it was easier for us to be each other's connections so we could have fun without the pressure of what-ifs.

But I couldn't help but feel slightly jealous of Lake, though it didn't make much sense that I would be jealous. Lake had been through hell before she and Nick finally got together. She deserved this happiness.

And I deserved to wait my turn.

"Anyway, I have a meeting, but do you want to stop by the café tonight? They're having a reading."

"I love that you opened up a vampire café in Denver."

Lake rolled her eyes. "The team opened up the café, I just helped back it. But now I get to deal with the press whenever they are afraid that real vampires roam the streets."

I shook my head. "They're idiots. Seriously," I added at her raised brows. "They really think that you are going to be drinking blood and turning victims into vampires at that place."

"Instead, we just serve sangria and cheese plates, while reading paranormal romance. I really don't know what the problem is."

"They need to get a life," I teased as I helped clear the table. There was staff for that, but since both of us had worked here at one point or another, we liked to make sure that the place was clean. We waved at our honorary aunt who owned the place and headed out.

"Are you headed into work?" Lake asked, her hand on her belly again.

I shook my head. "I'm headed to Clancy's."

"For second breakfast, you little hobbit?" Lake asked.

"I'm pretty sure you're already on your second breakfast, because baby needs fuel," I added quickly as she narrowed her gaze at me. "But Mom and Dad are there. Plus, I never get to see Amy," I said, speaking of my little sister.

"Good, sometimes I feel like we're all spread out all over the state, and it's hard to see our siblings."

That was true. Our parents were all cousins, technically, Lake and I were second cousins. It was just easier to call our generation the cousins. When we all started having kids though, that was going to get more complicated. It was honestly just easier to call each next generation cousins or siblings. I only had one sibling, while some of my cousins had three or four. It all worked out though, because we were a family. Always there for each other. Even if sometimes it was a little complicated because we were always in each other's business.

I hugged Lake goodbye, then headed to my car, grateful for the Montgomery parking lot. It was situated behind the original tattoo shop, and there was always a space for us if we got there in time. There were so many of us now though, that sometimes it was full. I headed out of town towards Arvada where Clancy's was located, which was also near Montgomery Security.

I had been raised in Colorado Springs, and that's where my parents and sister still lived. It was only an hour or so down I-25, with each of the suburbs of Denver and the major cities along the I-25 corridor feeling like one big city these days. My parents were up here meeting old friends, so I didn't have to drive down to Colorado Springs in rush hour and back. That would just set me on edge, considering most days it felt like it was taking more and more time to drive the highway. While I used the light rail as much as possible, usually I needed my car and all of my equipment, and therefore, I was stuck in a car more often than not.

I parked in front of Clancy's and made my way in, still full from breakfast, but I could probably fit in an iced latte with chocolate chips. That was my favorite thing here.

My parents were seated in a booth, sitting next to each other and laughing, while my sister sat on the other end shaking her head at their antics.

I loved my parents. I had always been a daddy's girl, even when my birth mother tried to take me away from him. And then when she had literally dropped me off on his doorstep, he took me in with no questions. I'd always known he was my safe space. I barely remembered my mom these days, and she didn't matter. She hadn't reached out, hadn't wanted to, and frankly I didn't either. Unless there was some health emergency and I needed her bone marrow or something, I didn't think I would ever contact her. There was no need.

Because I had my real mom. Adrienne Montgomery-Knight.

When Adrienne married my dad and officially adopted me, she took the last name Knight, moving Montgomery to one of her middle names, and I begged for the same. I wanted to be just like all of my cousins, I wanted to be a Montgomery.

They had said yes easily.

I hadn't been born a Montgomery, but I was made into one. I even had the same tattoo that most of the Montgomerys had. It was the Montgomery iris—an MI for Montgomery Ink, the tattoo shop and construction company that had branched out into who we were today. And surrounding that were irises, as well as some art. I loved it, it was the logo of the family, and it was put on everything we owned, which was starting to grow into an empire if you asked anyone outside the family. My mother had done my tattoo, scowling at my father and even Leif when they had asked to do it. No, my mom would, and it started a war over who was allowed to ink my skin. Were my aunts and uncles? My parents? My cousins? So many artists in the family, and that meant skin was real estate, a canvas made and honored.

"There's my girl," Mom said as she waved me over.

She wiggled out of the booth, my dad following her, and I hugged them tightly, my eyes watering for some reason. They had been so scared after the accident, after I'd almost died. They had wanted me to quit, to find a safer job. But I loved what I did. At least I thought I did.

My leg ached, and I was barely holding back a limp, but PT was working so, soon, I wouldn't even have that.

I held them tightly, and tried to reassure them through the hug that I was safe, before I let go and went to hug Amy. She was just out of college and looked so much like my mom it was a little startling. She had the Montgomery blue eyes, a wide smile, and looked model-gorgeous.

I was only a little jealous.

"You look great," Mom said as she and Dad took one side of the booth, and I took the other with Amy.

"Thanks, I try," I said with a laugh.

"So, you had breakfast with Lake already?" Amy asked.

I nodded. "Yes, but apparently I'm a hobbit today."

"Nothing wrong with that," she teased. The waitress came over and I ordered my coffee.

"I hope it's okay. We knew you were eating with Lake, so now you just get to watch us eat."

"And I got french fries with my club sandwich for breakfast," Amy added with a laugh. "So I'm sure you can have some."

"I knew I loved you for a reason."

"Well, at least there's that," she said with a roll of her eyes.

"So, have you thought about your next session?" Mom asked, not even bothering to ease into the conversation.

I rolled my eyes. "Yes, I want to go over the scars."

My mom's eyes went dark as my dad's hand tightened on his coffee mug.

I was usually a little more tactful than that, but I was tired and so in my thoughts these days, that I just blurted it like that.

"That's good, are you sure you're ready for that?" my dad asked before he held out his hand. He always had salt-and-pepper hair, even in his twenties, and now he was more salt than pepper. His beard was the same, and

I loved it. He looked just like my dad, like always. Maybe a little older, but still the favorite man in my life.

"Sorry, I didn't mean emotionally. We can talk about that if you'd like, but I actually meant physically. We don't know what the scars are going to look like in the next year or two."

I nodded, remembering the scars on my back. The explosion that had taken out the warehouse as I stepped out of it had not only fucked up my leg but had sent jagged pieces of metal into my flesh. My cousin had saved me, pulling me out before the fire reached me, but I'd still been bleeding a lot and had nearly died.

I nodded, saying my thanks to the waitress as she handed me my coffee and my family their breakfast. Grateful for the reprieve as they each settled their food in front of them, I let out a breath.

"The ones on my back are going to take more time, but the one on my leg? With the vitamin E oil and lotions I've been using, I think it's ready."

"So, I'll be doing it," my mom said with a tight nod, but my dad broke in.

"I don't think so. It's my turn."

"Really?" my sister whispered. "That's one way to get them off the subject."

I shook my head, loving the way that everybody fought over who was doing my tattoos, though nobody was really serious. It was our body so we could do what we wanted, but everybody was very territorial.

"I was actually thinking about Uncle Austin or Leif doing it. After all, Uncle Austin is world-renowned at doing tattoos over scarring." After all, that was how he had met his wife, my Aunt Sierra.

"Over my dead body," Adrienne Montgomery-Knight snapped, her eyes dancing with laughter. "I don't think so. It's my turn. If anyone's going to do that type of work, it's going to be me."

"Then I get your back," Dad said with a tight nod. "After all, I always have your back."

Amy groaned and I rolled my eyes. "Really?"

"Hey, one of the best parts of being a dad is the dad puns. I have a whole book of them. You got me that when you were six, and then another book later. Honestly, what more do I need?"

Thankful for the laughter, I sat back, stole a fry from Amy, and listened as my family talked about nothing important and yet everything. I was so grateful for them, and I knew that they were worried about me. Most people were. They saw me limp and were afraid I was remembering. Maybe that was the case. I did remember the fire, the screams, but I loved what I did. I loved protecting people, I loved making sure people felt safe in their own homes. So, while I might not be in the field as much right now, my strength was getting better, and I was almost ready. I just needed to make sure it never happened again. Which was what my job was about after all.

We talked about tattoos some more, and an upcoming family summit, and I checked my phone, realizing it was time for me to head out.

"I have to get to work. We have a meeting—a new hire."

"Look at you, taking over the world. I'm so proud of you." My dad squeezed my hand.

"We're trying. It's not easy to work for us, mostly because we fight like family, and some people don't get that."

"Then they aren't the right fit. But I hope this one works out. You guys need the people with how busy you're getting. Especially thanks to Ford's brothers."

I laughed at that, said my goodbyes, and headed to work.

I'd had a good weekend. It was a wedding that I hadn't wanted to go to, but I'd had a night that was perfect.

No promises. And while I might want a future, a forever, it wasn't going to be with some random man I met at a wedding who I was never going to see again.

I had things to do. Like remind my coworkers and family that I was damn good at my job and they didn't have to worry about me.

I just needed to make sure this new hire didn't have any qualms about working for my family, or the fact that all of us had our own drama.

When I stepped inside, everything ground to a halt. It was the same walls, the same windows, the same desks. The same back area where meetings could be held securely. There were the same family members, the same admin. Everything was the same.

Except it wasn't.

There was a man in a suit and a white button-down shirt standing next to Noah, a man that I knew very well.

He had brushed his red hair back from his face, and as he spoke to Noah, I heard the accent.

That damn British accent that had nearly made me come.

When he turned to me, his eyes widening, I blinked. This couldn't be real. Fate wasn't this cruel.

Noah looked between us, brow raised, curious as hell. "Hugh Hendricks, meet Daisy Montgomery-Knight, one of your bosses."

Hugh stood there while I blinked at him, wondering why the hell fate hated me so much.

Chapter Four

Hugh

They say dreams that are so vivid you could practically smell what was in the air were sometimes feasible. Yet, this didn't really feel like a dream. No, perhaps a nightmare, or irony and fate laughing their dirty little heads at me.

Because there she stood, the gorgeous and ineffable Daisy. The woman I had the best sex of my life with, was now apparently my boss.

She was just supposed to be the woman across the aisle, the woman I had been over and under, and now apparently was supposed to work under.

Fuck fate and all its irony.

I didn't know how she was going to play this. Was she going to pretend we didn't know each other? That we hadn't slept together?

I didn't know the politics behind this establishment, other than a group of friends and family owned the damn place and were the most sought-after security company in the area. Their rival company was actually trying to make waves against them, at least from what I remembered, but these were the people I wanted to work with.

That was why I had chosen this company, and not the other. I could have worked for the Shermans, but no, I had wanted to work with the Montgomerys.

And apparently I already knew one close up and personal.

Daisy moved forward, looking different than the woman in the short dress and wild hair. Instead, her hair was pulled back in a ponytail, her eyes fierce. She wore cargo pants and a tight T-shirt that showcased her breasts, even though it wasn't meant to be revealing. She had a cross body bag and work boots, and looked so damn sexy it was hard for me to breathe.

Dear God. I was going to hell or going to lose my job. This was great for day one. Hell, hour one.

This had to be a record.

Daisy held out her hand. "As he said, I'm Daisy Montgomery-Knight. You don't need to use all the names, though. Daisy will do. If we go by our last names, there'll be too many Montgomerys."

"Hugh Hendricks. I'm happy to be working here. I've heard great things."

"Well, that's good. We strive for the best reputation."

Noah looked between us, brow raised. He might not know what had happened, because we wouldn't be talking about any of that, but it was a little awkward when it was all I could do to not imagine her naked.

"Anyway, he starts training today." Noah cleared his throat. "Daisy was working on another project while we were doing the hiring, so she doesn't know your file as much as we do, so Kane's going to be your trainer."

Another Montgomery, although I didn't think his name was actually Montgomery. Was it Carr? Hell, I was trying to keep up with everyone, and yet all I could do was stare at Daisy.

This was going to be a problem.

"Hey, Hugh. We met during the interview process."

I nodded and shook hands with Kane. He was a big man with many tattoos and a fierce expression, but he could also laugh uproariously, as well as his cousin, Kingston.

I liked the people I'd met during the interview, and while I hadn't moved to Denver for this job, I was grateful for it all.

"Okay, let's finish up the introductions," Noah said,

clearing his throat. Everything felt so fucking awkward with Daisy, or perhaps that was just me. Because I wasn't looking at her, nor was she looking at me. This was going to be a problem. One we needed to figure out and work through. Just not right now. Not in front of everyone else.

"This is Ford, our other owner."

Ford, a man with dark hair and a long beard raised his chin at us, and I remembered that Noah and Ford were engaged. They were also with the owner of the café a couple of doors down, and I thought that was pretty cool. They seemed to be making it work, while I couldn't even get one relationship to work. But good on them.

"Ford and I do a lot of the behind-the-scenes things and the initial comps," Noah continued. "Kane and Kingston are major installers and do a lot of our body-guard work."

The two guys who looked more like twins nodded in unison, and I held back a smile at that.

"Gus and Jennifer are out on leave, and Jennifer will be working more in the office these days until she has her baby."

I raised a brow at that. "Is she the one that I saw yesterday?"

Noah shook his head. "No, that's our other cousin,

Lake. She owns her own company, as well as part of the tattoo shop next door."

I rubbed my temple. "How many cousins do you have?"

"Don't ask," the Montgomerys all said at once, while Ford just smiled into his coffee.

"Seriously, never ask that question. Because then more pop up."

"Says the man with how many siblings?" Noah asked, and Ford sighed.

"Let's not talk about that either." Ford met my gaze. "Let's just say there is a little more family than I was expecting," Ford said cryptically, and I raised a brow at Daisy, since she was the closest person to me, but she wasn't meeting my gaze. I could see the pulse in her neck beating rapidly, and I knew she was trying to figure out what to do.

Because this wasn't going to work. Sure, I would be working under Kane, but Daisy was my boss too. Wasn't she?

"Anyway, we all work on installing security systems, doing initial layouts, and going on one-on-ones. We're setting up new businesses right now and doing contracts that are requiring us to hire more, hence why you're here. We have a few contract workers who still get benefits through the company. But you'll be a full-time installer with us."

I nodded, having already agreed to this. He was probably going over all of this for the rest of the team.

Noah looked past my shoulder, and I turned to see another woman with dark hair and a bright smile walk in. "Hi, nice to see you again."

"Hello, Kate," I said to the admin as she went to her desk and immediately began answering phone calls. Ford and Kingston went back to work, and I stood there with Kane, Daisy, and Noah, feeling awkward as hell.

"As you can see, we are in and out most of the time, we have security briefings in the back where it is more secure. Ever since an incident last spring," he said, his jaw tensing, "we have higher security on the whole building. The family owns it."

My brows winged up. "So, are you guys like the Rockefellers or something?"

"Not even," Daisy said with a laugh, and I tried my best to ignore that laugh. I remembered the last time she'd laughed all husky like that.

"Anyway, I have to head into a meeting, but Kane and Daisy will handle you for the rest of the day. Welcome to the company."

Noah shook my hand again before he headed back to his desk to take a call. I nodded at Kane and Daisy. "Okay, I am ready when you are."

"I don't know if you're ready exactly for us. We're a

lot. We joke that we're taking over the world, but we're really not. We just happen to be a family-oriented business."

"If you say so. It is kind of nice that you all work together."

Daisy cleared her throat, and I was glad because I was afraid she was just going to stand there the whole time not saying anything, making things even more awkward.

"We try. We own this business, and our cousins work in the tattoo shop next door, well they own it, and then the women who own the café and bakery next to that are actually marrying into the family, so if we don't own something already, we just bring them into the family. Which sounds a lot more predatory than I meant."

"It's not predatory if it's true," Kane said with a laugh. "And then there's the art studio and galleria on the other side of that."

"It looked pretty cool, though I didn't get to go inside." I only had eyes for Daisy now, and it took all my effort to put them back on Kane. Luckily the guy didn't seem to notice. Or maybe that was just my wishful thinking.

"A lot of us just happened to go into a profession that required us to own our own businesses, and since our parents did the same, we learned from the best," Daisy said with a shrug. "I had things to do this morning, so did you get a tour?"

I shook my head. "This was about it. I had a few things to do this morning as well, so I'm just now starting." Like drop off Lucy at school and try not to feel like a horrible dad because I felt like I was fumbling around. This was my first school year as a full-time dad, and a single one at that. I was grateful Lucy was such a spark. I had to make sure she kept that spark.

Kane's phone rang and he looked down at the readout. "Hey, Daisy, can you give him a tour? I have to take this. Sorry, Hugh."

Before Daisy or I could respond, he quickly tapped his phone and started grumbling to whoever was on the line.

That left me and Daisy alone in the front of the shop, and while everyone else was around, no one was paying attention to us.

"Come on, I'll give you a tour of the outside first, and then we'll come inside."

I frowned at that but followed her out the front door and towards the other side of the building. It was a nice day out, not too hot, not too cold, and I could still see the mountains every time I looked west. It was a little shocking and something I wasn't used to. But it was damn gorgeous. Maybe I would become a hiker. I never really had the chance to while living in London or New York.

"Did you know?" she asked, and I turned to her.

"Did I know you were my boss? No. I have lines, Daisy. You might not know that, but I do."

"I didn't know either. I wasn't involved in hiring. I might be one of the owners on the door, but we each have our own parts of the company. That way we're not always second guessing and micromanaging. I didn't even know your name, only that we were hiring someone else."

"And then of course we only went by first names at the wedding."

Daisy cursed. "Damn it, damn it, damn it."

"We don't have to make this awkward. I promise I'm not going to sue you for sexual harassment."

"You could try, Ford's brothers could probably get that kicked out quite quickly."

"They're lawyers?"

"There're something," she mumbled. "Okay, this is what we're going to do. You're going to work hard, just like I know you will because Noah and Ford wouldn't have hired you otherwise. I'm going to work hard as well, but we're not going to work together. You're going to work for Kane, I'm going to work with my team, and we're not going to tell anyone what happened. It was just one night, and that's all it needs to be."

I raised a brow at her and nearly nodded right away, but there was something about this that made me want to take a minute. She was right. Everything she was saying was right. But I didn't like lying. And considering what these people did for a living, they were going to realize something was off. But perhaps we could talk it through.

"Your cousins are going to figure it out. You already acted weird when you first walked in."

"They've been watching me anyway; they already think that I'm acting weird for my own reasons."

I frowned. "Why?"

She waved it off. "There was an accident. I got hurt. I'm fine now. You're going to get all the details anyway, because we're still dealing with the aftermath of the explosion."

I nearly stepped forward to steady her, as if the explosion just happened. "But you're okay? Hell." I thought back to my hands on her body, those scars. "I was so damn rough with you."

She scowled, looking around as if someone was going to hear. That's when I realized we were standing right at the edge of the property, so the microphones from the cameras wouldn't be able to pick anything up. Smart. She was really damn smart.

"I'm fine. You didn't hurt me, and I wanted it just as

much as you did. You're the one that probably has fingernail marks all down your back."

I rolled my shoulders back, wincing. "You're right about that."

She smiled at me then, her eyes going smoky, and I couldn't help but smirk.

"We don't have to talk about it again though, because I have a feeling it's going to be harder to work together if we do."

She sobered at that. "You're right. But it's going to work—forget it ever happened and never talk about it again. I love my job, Hugh. I'm really damn good at it. And I'm healing, despite the fact that everybody seems to fucking worry about it."

"I remember your limp in your heels, I just thought it was your shoes."

She shook her head. "I go to PT. I'm fine, I promise. But they're going to worry over me, and I don't need them to worry over the fact that I slept with our new hire."

I winced at that. "And I don't want to be the guy who slept with his boss."

"Technically, even though I'm the owner, you're going to be working for Kane. So I'm not your boss. We have duty lines for a reason, mostly because Gus and Jennifer are together, and Ford and Noah are engaged. Things get complicated, so we always make sure that the person ahead of us is our team member, and not romantically involved."

"So, you're saying I have a chance," I teased, and she rolled her eyes. I was grateful she heard the humor. I did not have time in my life for complications like that. I had a new job, a new life, and Lucy. I didn't need to sleep with my boss. Or think about sleeping with my boss.

"Okay. We're coworkers, we had one night that we'll never talk about, and maybe one day we can be friends."

"I can do that. I've heard great things about this company, and I need this job. This new life. I'm not going to do anything to fuck it up." I scowled. "I'm not going to let you do that either."

I didn't mean to sound so accusatory, or maybe I did. I wasn't about to lose my job because things were awkward. Not when I hadn't even started yet. She seemed to think about that for a while before she held out her hand. I snorted, thinking how I had touched more than her hand. Only that was a thing for the past. So, I took her hand, shook it, and we nodded, holding on for a bit too long. I knew this was going to be a lot harder than we planned.

Because she told me she wasn't my boss, that she wasn't the one to sign my paychecks. She wasn't going to be the one training me.

But she was the one that had filled my dreams the

night before. She's the one I could still taste on my tongue.

And now I was going to work with her every single day.

This wasn't going to work. But I didn't have another choice.

So we were going to pretend. Only, I had a feeling pretending was only going to get us so far.

Chapter Five

Daisy

"One more set. You can do it."

"I hate you. With all of my heart I hate you. And I wish you would fall from that high horse you're on."

Crew rolled his eyes as he spotted me while I did my final squat.

When the bar was back on the rack, the weights off my shoulders, literally, not figuratively, I shook out my arms. "Why am I doing this again?"

"Because you want to be able to kick my ass?"

I raised a brow. "I think I can kick your ass without

having to do squats." Especially since my leg was killing me. I'd had PT in the morning and was allowed to work out like I was doing right now with Crew, but it wasn't easy. I was almost done with PT, almost done with all of these aches according to my doctors. Though I didn't believe them when my thigh still hurt and all I wanted to do was go to bed. Or kick my friend in the shin. Just because.

"You're a jerk, but don't worry, even if you think you can kick my ass, maybe you're just doing the whole workout thing so you can look hot."

I reached for my water and flipped him off as I took a swig. "Okay, there's so much wrong with that statement it's going to take me a few minutes to get through it. Either way, you're an asshole. And you dated me."

He grinned. "You were hot. But since you can kick my ass maybe that's why we broke up. Talk to me. What's really wrong?"

"You mean what's wrong in why I don't want to date you? Because we're better as friends. You know that." I winked as I said it, because I would rather talk about our failed relationship than anything real. Why did everybody want to talk about feelings? I might be a woman, I might like talking about my family's and friends' feelings, but that didn't mean I wanted to talk about mine. Especially to Crew. Because he had seen me naked.

"Shut up. Seriously though. What's wrong? Is it

your leg? I knew we were working too hard. If you get hurt again, your family's going to kick my ass. And while I know you could do it, so can your family. Even your little sister. She's very strong. It's quite frightening."

"I'm just in a funk." I sat down on the bench and watched Crew do arm curls, counting the reps with him. He didn't need a spotter, and frankly I was exhausted. I hadn't slept well the night before. Not because of stress or work or anything. No, it was all because of a certain British man.

Damn that new hire and the fact that he already haunted my dreams.

"Well, since you're in a grumpy mood today, let me make you grumpier."

I winced. "I'm not that grumpy, am I?" He gave me a look. "Okay, I *am* grumpy. I'm sorry."

"Don't apologize. You have a lot of reasons to be grumpy. Which brings up this next question." He took a deep breath, and I knew I wasn't going to like the next words out of his mouth. "Have they figured out who blew up the building?"

The building. The one that nearly killed me, where I had been flung to the ground, cut up, broken.

There had been only screams. My screams. And maybe Kingston's when he found me. I had been texting my cousin, Aria, to find out when she wanted to go on a girls' trip. I was on my way into the building to do an initial scope for a new security system.

I hadn't known it was wired to blow up.

I had thrown my hands over my face to try to protect myself from the flames. I miraculously wasn't burned. Kingston had pulled me out, burning himself in the process. He had a couple of scars on his arms, ones that would fade eventually, but the memory wouldn't. Not when he studied my face every once in a while, and I wasn't sure if he saw me or the memory of me lying on the ground, screaming in pain.

I hated that my cousin had to see that.

I wasn't the oldest of my generation. But I was one of the oldest. Leif and Lake were the two oldest, while I was third in line. The rest were a good five to fifteen years younger than us. I remembered Kingston as a baby. I remembered holding him when I was a little girl.

And then he was cradling me as we waited for the ambulance, stanching the bleeding.

It made me ill to think about—I didn't like to remember that day. But it kept being brought up. And hell, every time I had a twinge in my leg from working too hard, or if the weather changed, it reminded me as well.

So perhaps this was just my life now.

"Daisy?"

I looked down to see Crew kneeling in front of me, a concerned expression on his face.

I moved my fingers through his hair, pushing it back from his forehead. "I'm fine. Just grumpy I guess."

"Don't be grumpy, Daisy baby."

"Don't call me baby," I teased.

"I'll try." He stood up and went back to work. I shook my head, looking for a slight spark between us. It would be easier to fall for my friend than still have sex dreams about a man who now worked for me, with me, and had *really* worked against me.

Crew and I just didn't have that chemistry. We were friends, but it wasn't the same.

His best friend was actually my cousin Lex, who was slightly younger than us, but the two seemed to click. So Lex and Crew were always side by side, and the fact that Lex was out of town on a work trip was the only reason he wasn't in here working out with us, scowling at me just like Crew did if I winced when I worked out.

It would be easier to fall for Crew.

But I wasn't going to.

"Daisy, what the hell. What's going on in that mind of yours?"

"Just thinking that it would be easier if we actually liked having sex with each other."

He choked on the water he just drank and looked around the gym. I was grateful nobody seemed to overhear. Everyone had their earbuds in, working out to their own playlists. Crew just laughed. "You're ridiculous. And no, never again. It was fun, I mean you're pretty good at it."

"I'm fantastic," I teased.

"Sure, you are, babe. I am pretty sure that I'm the fantastic one and you had to rise to the occasion."

"Are you really going to use the word 'rise' in this conversation?"

"See, if we had any attraction to one another, I would be rising to the occasion from this conversation and yet, nothing." He looked down at his crotch.

I flipped him off. "Fuck you."

"That's the problem. We don't want to. Now, how many times are you going to change the subject. They never figured it out?"

"The authorities are still working on it. They know it was arson—a bomb—not an accident. They just haven't been able to tie it back to anyone."

"They don't still think it's you though, right?"

I shook my head. "Nope. Don't get me started again on that."

"What, the fact that they thought that the Montgomerys must have done it for the insurance money or something, just to not deal with the job?"

"We don't even get the insurance money. That's not how things work."

"I'm sorry. That's not my job. I'm just a lowly artist."

"Shut up," I said, exasperated. This was why we didn't work as a couple. We needled each other like siblings.

"Anyway, they don't know who did it. We might not ever know. But we're on alert, just like with all the incidents with our jobs."

"You have a dangerous job. There are going to be incidents."

I heard the worry in his voice, the same worry that echoed in my family's voices.

"I know, but I'm good at it. Even if I got blown up."

"Let's not talk about that again. I'm going to have to hurt someone just thinking about it."

"Same." My phone buzzed and I scowled as I pulled it out of my pocket.

"What is it?" Crew asked, curious as ever.

Noah: *Meeting at 8:00. Sherman Priority Security has a new offer.*

He added an eye roll emoji, and I sighed.

"Sherman is back at it."

"That rival security company?" Crew asked.

"I wouldn't call them a rival. They do decent work, but there are no women other than in the office. Only dudes jacked up on steroids who think that they need to protect the little lady. They're strapped to the nines when they go out, and it's ridiculous."

"And they want to buy you out? Why?"

"Because we get some clients they want. But they get some clients we want. It's what happens when you're competing in business. Plus, they take the clients we don't want."

"The assholes?"

"The assholes. Like the ones that try to use 'security' as a way to hit on people that work for them." I used air quotes around security, and Crew rolled his eyes. "There was this one client that constantly hit on Jennifer and me and nearly locked us in a back room with the owner." Crew's eyes darkened. "It's fine, we took care of ourselves. And then we fired them. But they hired Sherman. So now Sherman wants to either merge with us, which sounds disgusting, or buy us outright. No, thanks."

"So you need a meeting to discuss that?"

"Yes, but I'm pretty sure the meeting is going to be about how we get the hell away from them. It will be fun."

"Sounds like it." We cleaned up our area before we headed to the locker room. After I was showered and dressed, I piled my hair on the top of my head, not bothering to blow it out. I'd shower in the morning and I wasn't in the mood to deal with it tonight.

Crew met me in the lobby and raised a brow. "So, are we going to talk about the other thing?"

I frowned, my stomach rumbling. I was hungry and wasn't in the mood to cook. Plus, I wasn't sure I even had anything in my house to make a meal out of.

"What are we talking about?" I asked, distracted.

"The fact that I didn't see you after you scampered away to your room with a certain British heartthrob."

My head shot up. "What?"

"I saw that. I saw you leave. You didn't even say goodbye, Daisy."

Realization slammed into me and I cursed. "Oh my God. I can't believe I forgot."

"You forgot me so easily. I should be offended, but I'm not. Now, do you want to tell me how it was?"

"We are not that close, Crew," I said with a nervous laugh.

"Maybe not, but I do have questions."

I froze and met his gaze. "What kind of questions?"

"About how it feels to work with him." He grinned then, as if he had been keeping a secret for so long and it felt so good to finally let it out.

I looked around nervously, as if one of my family members was going to hop out from behind a corner at any minute. And with the number of family members I had, that could actually happen. They could be here, waiting. They wouldn't even have to try to spy, they could be here because we all lived near each other and that was what happened when my family procreated.

"How the hell did you know that?" I spat, keeping my voice low.

"I saw him coming out of Latte on the Rocks when I was going in. Then I saw him talking with Noah about work and assumed he was the new hire. I recognized him from the way you two were plastered all over each other on the dance floor. I have so many questions."

I pulled him out the door, towards the car, trying to make sure nobody saw us. "You cannot tell anyone. We are not telling anyone."

Crew's brows shot up. "Really? You're going to keep the fact that you had a one-night stand with your new hire hidden? I don't see that blowing up in your face at all." He winced. "Sorry for using that turn of phrase."

I waved him off. "It's fine. I'm not going to cry when you say 'blow up.'" I winced. "Okay, maybe I will, but later. Promise me you're not going to tell anyone about what happened with Hugh. Or that you know anything about him. Don't even talk to him. Don't mention him. Ever."

"I'm not going to bring it up, nor will I tease you or Hugh about it. I promise." I trusted Crew when he made a promise. Because he was a good guy, even if he meddled in my affairs, just like my family did. "Please, though, think about it. It's going to be complicated."

"We already said it wasn't going to be complicated. We talked about it."

Crew sighed. "In other words, you told him not to say anything and he agreed to it because you are demanding?"

"Why does that make me sound like a bitch?"

"That makes you sound like you're trying to protect yourself and Hugh. Just, be careful, Daisy. I care about you." He held up a hand. "As your friend. Like we've discussed often. I'm not carrying a flame for you." He winced. "How many fire and bomb references are in our everyday language?"

I waved him off. "Thank you. Seriously. We'll figure it out. It's fine. It was just one time, and it's never going to happen again."

Crew didn't look like he believed me, but he leaned down and kissed my cheek. "Be careful. With him and you." Then he got in his car, and I sighed before climbing into mine.

My stomach still rumbled but worry eked in over it. What the hell was I going to do? First thing, I was going to eat, and then pretend everything was fine. Because it had to be. There was no other option.

I pulled into my favorite Indian restaurant to order my favorite meal. Garlic naan, a lamb samosa, a chickpea samosa, and goat korma. My mouth watered just thinking about it.

While waiting for my meal, I turned and nearly dropped my phone.

He was there. How the hell was he there?

He sat at a table and nodded at something his partner said. I blinked when I noticed that it wasn't an adult sitting in front of him, but a little girl. One with the same auburn hair and bright smile as Hugh.

It seemed as if the floor had fallen out from beneath me before Hugh turned and noticed me.

Well, it wasn't like I could slink out of there, not after he knew I was here.

He cleared his throat and waved, and the little girl looked at me and smiled brightly.

"Hi!" the little girl said quickly. She had an American accent, not a British one, and that confused me. She looked so much like Hugh, but maybe this wasn't his daughter? He hadn't told me he had a daughter. Hell, I didn't know anything about him. I had purposely not looked up anything at work either, because I hadn't wanted to cross any boundaries. He was in Noah's and Kane's department. Not mine.

I was oddly angry he hadn't told me, but when would he have? When he had his tongue in my mouth?

Hugh stood up and awkwardly cleared his throat. "Daisy. I must have picked a good place if the locals are here."

I smiled awkwardly. "It's my favorite place. I just ordered takeout."

"Daddy, is this Daisy? Your boss?" Lucy asked, and a few things all hit me at once.

Daddy. This was Hugh's daughter.

Where was this little girl's mother? Had I slept with a married man? Oh God. Why was this so complicated?

And she knew my name. That I worked with him. What else had he told this child?

I was usually good with children, but it felt like I was tongue tied.

Hugh looked between us. "Yes, Lucy, sorry. Daisy, this is my daughter, Lucy. Lucy, this is Daisy. We work together."

"She's your boss. I like that you have a lady boss. There should be more lady bosses."

That made me smile, and Hugh's lips twitched as well.

"I think there should be too."

"Do you want to eat with us? You should. You should eat with us. I really like samosas. And curry. And spicy."

Hugh looked like he'd rather be anywhere but here. Well, that was fine. I wanted the floor to open up and take me down with him. But that wasn't going to happen.

"Oh, don't worry. I'm fine."

"Ms. Daisy, I saw you have friends here, so I put everything in bowls for you to eat at the table. Join them. You should join them," the manager said as she gave me a pointed look.

I knew that there was no getting out of this. She would tell my mother if I was rude, or if I was ignoring a man. She would probably tell my mother that I was eating with a man anyway. That was the problem when you went to mom-and-pop shops where they knew your family. They told them everything.

"Please join us."

Between the smile on his face as he looked at his daughter, the fact that I didn't really have a choice, and the fact that I had limped over there because my leg was aching, I realized I couldn't turn the invitation down. I sighed and smiled. I was a damn glutton for punishment.

And I was starving.

"That sounds lovely. It's nice to meet you, Lucy."

"It's nice to meet you too, Daisy."

I sat down next to Hugh, doing my best to ignore the heat of him.

And doing my best to pretend that this wasn't a dumb idea.

Chapter Six

Hugh

This was not how I had expected to spend my evening with my daughter, but I should have known that my luck wasn't that good. That, added to the fact that Lucy never knew a stranger.

Daisy sat next to me, her arm brushing mine whenever she reached for her meal. We had a simple meal of butter chicken and vindaloo, as well as naan, but we hadn't gotten the garlic butter version that Daisy had.

"Does that have cheese on it?" Lucy asked, and I pulled my attention back to what was happening in front of me, and not on the fact that the woman I'd slept with was now sitting in front of my daughter, and I could feel the heat of her skin against mine.

This woman was my boss. I had to remember that.

"You got the regular naan, which is amazing, and I could eat the entire basket of it. I got the garlic cheesy naan. So, if you spread it apart like this, you get to see all the cheese." She proceeded to show Lucy by tearing the naan in half, and we watched as the gooey cheese spread out in the most delicious thing I had ever seen in my life. My mouth actually watered.

"Oh, wow. Daddy, we should have gotten that."

I winced. "Next time. I'm sorry, this is our first time here, and I wasn't sure what we would like."

I knew what I liked with Indian food, I ate it all the time in New York, but I wasn't sure about my daughter. Not that I was going to get into that with Daisy here. Lucy didn't need to know my guilt either. I had seen the surprise on Daisy's face when she realized I had a kid. I didn't bring Lucy up in conversation. My private life was private for a reason, and in my line of business it was always helpful to keep your life out of conversation. Nobody needed to know about my kid. And hell, I didn't need the complication of Daisy wondering about my personal life. Not that anything was complicated at all. No, this was fine.

"You can have some now," Daisy said with a grin on her face. "Is that okay?" she asked me, and I nodded.

"You don't have to give us all of your dinner."

Daisy grinned and tore the naan up a bit more so we

could each have a piece. "Oh, you don't get all of it. Sorry, that's not how this works."

"Thank you so much," Lucy said, a huge grin on her face. She took a bite and her eyes nearly rolled in the back of her head. She grinned up at Daisy and bounced on her seat. "This is so good. Thank you."

"You're welcome. I love all kinds of naan." Daisy took another bite, and I had to tear my gaze away at the sight of her eating.

I was a sick, sick man.

I quickly stuffed a piece of the cheesy garlic naan in my mouth and groaned; this had to be one of the best things I'd ever eaten. I loved Indian food, but this place? Hands down the best.

"What is that?"

"It's goat korma," Daisy said. "Have you ever had goat?"

Lucy shook her head and looked at me. "Have I?"

"You haven't. But it's actually really good. We got chicken this time because it's your first time here. I wanted to go with something that I know you like."

"You're welcome to try this too," Daisy said, gesturing to her meal.

I cleared my throat. "Again, you don't have to share everything, but thank you. And you're welcome to ours. We're not going to be able to finish this anyway. Even though this little one could probably eat me out of house and home."

Lucy beamed, and I reached across the table with my napkin, wiping the smear of sauce off her face.

"I love food. Thank you, Daddy."

"You're welcome, baby," I whispered, and I could feel Daisy's eyes on me. She probably had so many questions. But it wasn't the time or the place.

Plus, I didn't want to think about my ex, or why I lived here.

"Oh, this is so good," Lucy said as she tried the goat, and I just laughed, watching her eat.

"Not hungry?" Daisy asked, her voice low, and I cleared my throat, turning my attention back to Daisy.

"Sorry, just got distracted. It's good seeing her happy." I whispered the last part, hoping Lucy wouldn't hear.

Daisy gave me a curious look, but I shook my head. I wasn't ready to go over everything. Though maybe I should.

Maybe it would be good for everyone if I finally did.

"By the way, is your leg okay?" I asked quietly, and I couldn't help but notice that she froze at the question.

"I'm fine," she said sharply, and I cursed under my breath.

"Sorry. It's none of my business. You're just in gym

clothes and limping. I thought maybe you hurt yourself at your workout."

"What was your workout?" Lucy asked, and I shook my head.

"Don't talk with your mouth full, baby."

"Sorry, Daddy," she said with a grin before she swallowed the rest of her food.

"Good job."

"It's really good food though. You should be eating."

"Yes, you should be eating," Daisy said pointedly before she took a bite of her food and smiled over at Daisy.

"I was boxing and working on some stretching. A few weights. No cardio for me today."

"I like cardio. Because then I can play soccer with my friends. Although Daddy calls it football." She rolled her eyes dramatically in only the way a five-year-old could.

"I'll have you know that it's called football around the rest of the world. I'm sorry that you Americans don't understand."

"But I'm half-American and half-British. I can call it both." Lucy beamed, and I couldn't help but grin. Damn it, I loved my kid.

"You're right. But at least in my company, call it football."

"If I have to."

She sighed dramatically again before digging into her food. She seemed to like the goat and chicken equally, and I added that to my mental notes of her likes and dislikes.

"My cousin Kingston calls it football too. And always gets on us when we call it soccer. Even though he's born and raised in Colorado," she told Lucy.

"Really? I wonder why that is."

"I think he was just trying to needle his siblings and cousins, and now it just turned into a thing. You know family. We're complicated but love each other."

I nodded, knowing how complicated family could be.

It took a while, but finally I relaxed, even though I could still feel the heat of Daisy at my side. We ate, Lucy taking second helpings and I wondered where it all went. But she was happy, full, and getting all of her vitamins and minerals. What more could a father ask for?

By the time we finished and paid, her eyes were drooping.

"Let's take the rest home for leftovers, and then we'll get you home, baby girl. You've had a long day."

"I really like school, and I like my classes and my teachers, and I met a new friend named Nora. She's the greatest."

Daisy blinked and frowned. "Nora Montgomery?"

Lucy's eyes widened and she giggled. "Yes! Nora Montgomery. She's the sweetest person ever. And I met Molly and Shane, who are Nora's best friends. And they said that though they're all best friends, they always have room for more friends. I was really sad to leave my other friends, but everybody's new at school anyway so it's okay."

I looked over at Daisy and raised a brow. "Montgomery? Let me guess, a cousin?"

Daisy laughed, shaking her head. "Oh God, I love the fact that my family seems to be collecting friends like a spider in its web."

"Spiders are scary," Lucy said, and I reached across the table to squeeze her shoulder.

"You're fine. She doesn't mean it in a bad way." I looked over my shoulder at Daisy, who winced.

"I promise it's a good thing. Nora is my cousin Sebastian's daughter. Sebastian works in the tattoo shop next door," she told me, and I nodded.

"I guess that makes sense. Well, small world."

"But I thought you said the world was big. And that's why Mommy can't visit." Lucy's words brought me out of my staring at Daisy and I nearly cursed.

"You're right. It is a very big world. By small world I meant the fact that you already met one of Daisy's family members. Isn't that great?"

"I guess. Nora's really nice." She yawned hard, and I ran my hand through her hair.

"Let's get you home and into bed. But let's brush those teeth first."

"Okay. I like brushing my teeth. I have a whole song." We packed up our leftovers and headed towards our cars, Lucy lagging at my side. I picked her up, loving the way she nestled her head onto my shoulder, conking out before we even made it to the car.

"Oh, to be that young and to fall asleep anywhere."

I was grateful my car unlocked itself as soon as I stood by it. I set the food down on the floor behind the passenger seat, and somehow tucked Lucy into her car seat without waking her up. Of course, that kid could probably sleep through a hurricane, so what did I know?

"So, I guess I should thank you for inviting me to dinner," Daisy said after a minute, and I closed the car door, cracking open the driver's side door so I could hear Lucy if she needed me.

"I am sorry. I mean, I know this is probably not how you wanted to spend your evening, listening to my daughter talk a mile a minute. It's really hard keeping up with her." I ran my hand through my hair as I met Daisy's gaze.

She looked so damn sexy. Maybe because she had just worked out and then spent the evening making my kid laugh.

Damn it, this was going to be a problem.

"Your kid's the sweetest. And Nora? That kid is

amazing. I've loved that little baby since the moment I held her." She cleared her throat. "Nora's mom died in childbirth at only eighteen. My cousin Sebastian was nineteen when Nora was born. So, we as a family have done our best to make sure that Nora knows she's loved, and that her family loves her. Now Sebastian's going to marry one of my good friends, Raven—she owns the café in our building."

My heart ached for Nora, Sebastian, and the rest of them. "I can only imagine that pain. I'm so sorry. Sorry for Nora and all of you. That's rough."

"It is. It was. But Nora is loved, and they talk about Marley, her birth mom, often. That way she'll always remember her even though she never got to meet her." Daisy's voice roughened before she cleared her throat. "Lucy's the sweetest." She paused for a minute, cleared her throat again, awkwardly this time. "Should I ask about her mom?" Then she held up her hand. "Sorry. I guess as your boss, that's straying way too far."

I shook my head, letting out a hollow laugh that didn't have much humor in it. "Daisy, nothing about who we are is normal. We're not going to fit ourselves in a little box. We've known that since our first dance."

"Hugh," she began, and I shook my head.

"No. I'll talk about her." I looked over my shoulder and made sure Lucy was asleep. "I came to New York over five years ago for a bachelor party."

Daisy raised a brow. "You flew across the ocean for a bachelor party?"

"It was my brother's bachelor party. Our family comes from money and my brother liked to spend it. Still does, mind you. So we flew to New York so we could have a drunken revelry." I sighed and rolled down the window a bit, then clicked the door shut. I could hear my kid if she needed me, but hopefully she couldn't hear me. Thankfully her being a hard sleeper would make it unlikely she would hear any of this.

"I met Cheryl that night. We had fun. Probably too much fun." I put the emphasis on the word fun, and Daisy nodded.

"I see."

"Cheryl got pregnant, and I decided to move to New York to try to figure out how to be a father."

"So, you and Cheryl were together?" Daisy asked, her voice low.

"We got married, because I thought we fit. I was wrong. My ex-wife wasn't happy about being a mom. She wasn't happy about anything. She wanted to go out and party and enjoy life. I tried to file for divorce because I wanted to be a good dad who didn't actively hate his child's mother, and things got complicated. We'd been married for three years, so I got a green card and eventually got dual citizenship. All so I could live here and be near my kid. And when it came time to fight for custody,

I was in the precarious position where I was working too-long hours owning my own security business. Cheryl got full custody."

"That bitch," Daisy grumbled, and I laughed.

"You're right about that, and you don't even know the half of it. Because then Cheryl got what she wanted. She found a man with more money than me."

Daisy's eyes widened. "You've got to be kidding me."

"Nope. I got to see my kid on some weekends, barely got to see her at all. I was trying to figure out how to be a dad when I wasn't even allowed to see my kid. Then Cheryl got remarried, and the man happened to get a new job out here in Colorado."

"So you moved here to be with your kid? But how do you have custody now?"

Rage settled in me, and I slid my hands in my pockets. "Cheryl decided to start over. It wasn't going to be easy for her to start a new family, a new life in the society circuit, when she had a kid from her old marriage. So she decided to give me full custody."

Daisy began to pace, letting out a few curse words that seemed to take someone's anatomy and twist it on its end. I agreed wholeheartedly with her, but I had to let go of the rage. If I didn't, it would twist me up inside, and I had to be the better person. I had to protect my kid. And I wasn't going to be able to do that if I hated her mom.

"So now you're a full-time dad, and you moved out here for what, to be near a woman who doesn't even want her daughter? That doesn't make any sense to me."

I sighed and ran my hands through my hair. "I needed to start over. I needed a job where I wasn't working long hours running a business. I couldn't keep owning my own business in a city where the price of living is astronomical. I couldn't keep living in a place that didn't have a yard for my kid to grow up in and play. I wasn't from New York. I'd only lived there to be near Cheryl and Lucy. And when Cheryl decided to move out here, I knew I was going to drop everything anyway. It just made sense. And then once we all moved out here, she decided she didn't want custody at all. So, she signed Lucy over, and I found myself in a quandary. Where do I start over?"

"And you started over where Lucy could maybe see her mom. If her mom ever got her head out of her ass."

I snorted. "Pretty much. It hasn't happened yet, but you never know. I heard good things about your company, about your family, and I figured why not start here. I couldn't take my daughter back to London. Not when the legal ramifications could get complicated. Maybe one day we'll move there, but right now this is where we need to be. So, I'm figuring out how to be a dad. A single dad at that. I'm just really glad that you guys have good childcare as part of the benefits."

Daisy smiled, and I hadn't realized how close we were, so close that I only needed to lean down to brush my lips against hers. Damn it, this was a problem.

"Well, I'm glad we can help with that. And I guess that answers my question about why you came to work for us instead of working on your own."

I reached out and pushed her hair back from her face, wondering why as I did it. Wondering when I should stop.

Her tongue darted out to lick her lips, and I did what I shouldn't. I lowered my mouth to hers and kissed her.

Her hands went to my chest but not to push me away. They sat on my chest, the heat of her sliding through the cotton of my shirt. It was as if she wanted to push me away and pull me towards her at the same time. I kissed her softly, a little sweetly, and then pulled back, pressing my forehead to hers.

"Shit."

"Yep."

"Shit," I repeated. "But I want to do it again." I hadn't meant to say that out loud, and I knew that was probably going to bite me in the ass.

"Same."

Oh, this was going to be a problem. I did not have time for this in my life. It was going to be complicated, and no matter what, it was going to end badly.

"So, what if we do it again?"

She stiffened, and I was afraid I had said something wrong. Maybe she would be smart and walk away. Because that was what we should do.

"Just not at work," she said quickly, and all of my thoughts that she would walk away vanished, buried under the excitement of what could be.

"Not at work," I agreed.

"Kane is training you, but technically I'm still your boss."

"Noah signs the checks. Kane is training me. And we already decided that I'm not really working under you."

Of course, I wanted to be under her, but I wasn't going to make that joke.

"Still," she said with a laugh.

"We'll figure it out."

I pulled away so I could study her face and she gave me an odd smile.

"Maybe. You should go get your daughter to bed, and we'll give each other some time to figure out how big of a mistake we're making." She patted my chest before she walked back to her car, only two spaces away, and sighed.

Well, shit.

Chapter Seven

Daisy

All I could think about was the coffee currently sliding through my system. Okay, perhaps that wasn't all, because Hugh's words from the night before were also sliding through my memory.

Lucy's story reminded me so much of my own that it took me a moment to break through that barrier when he explained it.

What was it about mothers? Why couldn't they just love you and keep you? Why were you always second best?

I hated that I even asked myself that question, but it

was the truth. I hadn't been chosen. My mother left me on my father's doorstep and never looked back. She gave up custody and had not once reached out or even sent me a birthday card. I hadn't needed presents or money or anything from her. I just wanted a hug from my mom and hadn't understood why she didn't love me enough to stay.

My mother left me for a better position, for her dream job. For a career that changed lives.

And she changed mine, like leaving behind a forgotten sock that could never find its mate.

I had been lucky, so damn lucky that my father took me in. Of course, that was a silly thing to think. My father had always fought to keep me. To be the best dad he could be. He hadn't even thought twice about becoming a full-time dad. Just like Adrienne had stepped up to the plate, and become my friend, my confidante, my mother.

I had no idea where my mother lived now, what she was doing, if she had ever gotten married again or had other kids. I didn't care. Maybe part of me should, but I didn't.

That was on her, and maybe one day when I wasn't so angry about what she had done to me and my family, I would reach out. Or maybe I would look her up to see what she was doing.

Lucy had been left behind as well, but Hugh was

stepping up to the plate and changing his life to make sure his daughter was loved.

It surprised me that he moved to Colorado just to be near a woman whom he clearly didn't love, and who didn't seem to love her own daughter. He was doing what he thought best for his little girl. And just like me, she was young enough to see the happiness, but she would always know. She would always know that her mother hadn't loved her enough to stay. And I prayed that she would be strong enough to realize her father loved her enough. That it wasn't her that was found lacking.

It had taken me years to understand that. To let myself believe it. My parents had done their best to try to instill that in me. Hell, the entire Montgomery clan, as well as all of my other aunts and uncles, had always been there to protect me. To make sure I knew I was worthy of love and happiness. But it had taken a little bit longer than that, a little bit more therapy, to let myself believe it.

Maybe I would talk to Hugh about that.

Not that I needed to dump my trauma on him. And not something I needed to share with him considering we had kissed.

Damn it, we had kissed, and it was amazing, and we were going to do it again. There was no mistaking that.

It was going to cross lines and neither of us needed that in our lives.

I really wanted to kiss him again.

"Earth to Daisy."

I shook myself out of my thoughts and looked over at Raven and Greer. Considering I was in their café, and they were taking time to sit with me for a quick breakfast, I should probably pay attention to them, rather than my own thoughts.

"Sorry. What were you saying?"

"No, we want to know what you're thinking."

I shook my head. "Everything's fine. Just in need of this caffeine." I took a sip of the caramel latte that Greer made for me while she studied my face.

"Long night?" she asked, the implication in her tone undeniable.

"I had Indian food. It was really good."

She kept waiting for more, but I wasn't in the mood to share. After all, we said we would keep it to ourselves.

I wasn't about to make a liar out of myself.

"So, I hear there's a new hire a couple of doors down," Raven said.

I narrowed my gaze at her, wondering what she had heard.

"Oh, you mean the British heartthrob," Greer said, her hand over her heart. "He's so dreamy."

"Don't you have two men too swoon over? How many more do you need?"

She flipped me off, not even offended.

"Oh, Noah and Ford are enough for me to handle. Believe me."

I shuddered. "Noah is like my brother. Ford is too. Not sure I need that in my mind."

"Look who brought it up. Oh, maybe that was me." Raven winked and I rolled my eyes.

"I really need to get into work and actually focus on my day."

Raven met my gaze. "Do you need to talk? About anything?"

I loved Raven. I loved that she was becoming part of this family and was someone I could trust. But I didn't know what to say. What I was feeling. So I just smiled and shook my head.

"Thank you for the coffee and Danish. Now I'm going to go save the world."

"That's what I love about you. Always so gentle and cautious."

I rolled my eyes and hugged her, before waving at Greer, who was back behind the counter, and headed over to the office.

It was early enough that not everybody was there. Some of the team went directly to their job sites rather than coming to the office first. I knew Noah and Ford were on an overnight. They didn't usually do jobs together because of the conflict of interest, but this one was a special case. Some events required us to stay with a client for more than twenty-four hours. Noah and Ford were the best at those long jobs, and I was pretty damn good too. However, I really didn't enjoy doing overnights when it was a group of only men. While it shouldn't be a problem, in my job it always could be. Men didn't trust that I could handle myself.

I went inside and smiled at Kate, who was on the phone, busily typing. I really liked Kate; she was a great addition to the team. We needed somebody to organize us and keep us running, and Kate not only had the experience, she could handle us. It wasn't that we were ridiculously annoying or inappropriate. It was because we were family that worked together. And while that meant we would always be there for each other, it also meant that she had to deal with us acting like family. We were a lot to handle, even on a good day. But Kate handled us like a pro.

Jen was also there, leaning back in her seat, her hands on her rounded belly. I couldn't believe the other woman on our team was working while pregnant. Not that she couldn't handle it, but she had been so sick for her first trimester that I was afraid for her even being able to stand up without being nauseous. But she was doing great, and worked from the office more days than not, and I knew that her new husband, Gus, who also worked for us, was happy with that arrangement. He was out with Noah and Ford, and struggled when his wife was in the line of duty. He was getting over that though —he had to. It gave me hope that Jen and Gus could work that out.

Not only were they not allowed to work together on certain assignments, just like any couple wasn't, Gus also trusted her to take care of herself. Which reminded me that every single guy I dated recently thought I couldn't handle myself. They wanted to protect the little lady and they couldn't handle the fact that I could take care of myself.

I wasn't sure how I'd find a person that understood what I did. I loved my job, even though sometimes I questioned why I did. I was damn good at it. I just wished I could find someone who understood that.

And because fate hated me, I looked up just as Kane and Hugh came in from the back talking in serious tones, and I tried my best not to react to Hugh. I worked with some of the most observant people in our field. I had a feeling that us lying about knowing each other and having been with each other was probably a mistake. But I hadn't thought of another way to handle it. They were going to figure us out. They always would. There was no hiding the way I looked at him, so I didn't look at him.

"Daisy, can you come look at this?" I held back a curse at Kane's words and smiled brightly as I walked over to them, trying not to act as if I wanted to reach out and brush Hugh's hair from his face.

I'd never done that before, why would I want to now? There was something wrong with me.

"What's up?" I asked.

Kane handed me the paperwork he was holding. "We have an installation today; do you want to come with? I don't know what's on your plate."

I ignored the knee-jerk reaction to say no because it had nothing to do with work. I wasn't sure how to act around Hugh. Because I'd had dinner with his daughter. And it was nice. I wasn't sure what I was supposed to do now.

"Yeah, I can look at it."

Kane looked up at me, studying my face. "I heard back from Detective Johnson again, by the way," he said, as Hugh looked between us, interest in his gaze.

I stiffened at the mention of that man's name but nodded.

"Anything?"

"No, but he's probably going to want to talk to you again. And Kingston."

"Is Detective Johnson worried about the company?" Hugh asked, and I shook my head. There was no use hiding everything like this from him because he needed to know the dangers. Hell, he knew them. He had been in situations like this before. I had read his file that morning, finally realizing that trying to keep distance between us wasn't going to work. I needed to deal with the fact that I had slept with Hugh, and part of me wanted him again. And that he'd kissed me, and I'd kissed him right back. I didn't know what was going to happen next, but we were going to have to work it out.

"It's about the explosion at the warehouse. Detective Johnson is lead detective on it, but I guess there's nothing to detect. No leads at all."

Hugh shook his head. "Seriously? After all this time?"

For some reason, him being as angry as I was soothed me.

"Pretty much. Between that and Sherman Priority Security trying to buy us out every other week, I'm done with paperwork and useless meetings."

"Do you mind if I look at the file?"

Hugh was looking at me, not Kane, and I couldn't help but stare right back.

"No, but I don't know what you're going to see that we haven't."

"I'm an outsider. I wasn't connected to it. And I'm angry that you were hurt, and Kingston could have been hurt. I want to see what happened."

"Sure," I said, lying. I didn't want anyone to read the report, because photos of me were in there. Of what made my scars. Scars he felt, kissed, but I didn't want him to see the initial injuries. But everyone else in this company, including Kate, had read the file. If there was something that he could gain from it, then I wished him the best of luck.

"I don't know what you're going to get from it, but if you figure it out that'd be fucking great." Kane shook his head. "I'm tired of our family getting hurt."

"Same," I said with a sigh.

"Okay, I appreciate it. And I am just as pissed off as you guys. Nobody gets to hurt our team."

Kane grinned at that. "Look at you, fitting in already. I love it. Anyway, here's the file on where we're going today. You up for it?"

I nodded as I looked at my phone for my schedule. "I'm going to drive separately though; I have an installation this afternoon. Long day."

"Those are the best kinds. That means clients."

"Hear, hear," Jen said from her desk before she went back to typing.

I grinned, ignoring the feel of Hugh's gaze on me. This was going to be a problem. Or perhaps it already was.

Because I hadn't told him. I hadn't said what I wanted. I didn't know what we were going to do about this attraction that would not go away.

I got an hour of paperwork in before I followed

Kane and Hugh to the job site. It was a simple installation at a business. We did bodyguard work as well as installations. We were good at what we did.

"I know you've done this before, but let's make sure we have everything up to code for Colorado versus New York."

Hugh grinned. "I like the mountains better than the city view. There I've said it," Hugh said with a laugh.

There was something about that British accent that nearly sent me over the edge. I needed to focus on work though, not Hugh.

I was on one side of the building, while Hugh and Kane were on the other, and I couldn't help but notice how quick Hugh was, and he was damn good. He was great working with the clients, and also quick to focus and get things done. He was a good hire, and he'd be great for the team. I just needed to get my hormones in check.

We moved to the back of the lot when Kane looked at his phone and cursed.

"What is it?" I asked.

"I need to head to Dr. Allen's office."

Hugh looked confused when I cursed under my breath. "Are you serious? What does he want this time?"

"Not sure, but he's a high-paying client, so that means I need to go and fix it. He was probably fucking with it, but there's nothing I can do."

I shook my head but understood.

"Are you heading out now?"

Kane gave me a pained look, but I knew there wasn't another option. There were three of us at this installation, and we didn't need all three of us. But that meant I'd be left alone with Hugh. Great.

"I'm sorry. We both know that I can't fuck up with this guy. He has connections. And he's picky."

"We're good. I can head back with Daisy when we finish, if that's okay?" Hugh looked at me, and I nodded.

"It's fine. We've got it."

Kane headed out, leaving me alone with Hugh.

He gave me a look, and I continued to work in silence.

"Are we just not going to talk?" he asked.

I sighed and went back to the readout on the digital pad. "I'm just working. You're good though." I looked up at him and smiled. "Seriously. You must have done this before."

"I used to own my own business. You know that."

I nodded and went back to work.

"I'm still confused why you're working for us, rather than starting a business here."

He laughed at that. "You want more competition? Funny way of being a boss. Honest answer? I wanted to spend more time with my kid."

"I like that. It's a good answer."

"I was a good boss. But I was also the only boss. I only had a couple of guys working for me, so if there was an issue, it was me on the line. It was me spending too much time dealing with the politics. Which is fine. I liked it, I loved it even, and I was damn good at it."

"But that left no time for Lucy."

"Bingo. I only took off the weekends I had her. The team understood, but it's not the same."

"I get it. And I am glad you're there for Lucy. You're a good guy."

He snorted and shook his head. "Or it just makes me an idiot for selling my business and starting over."

"Come on, you want me to drop you back at the office?"

"Sure. Unless you want me at that next installation?"

"No, I can handle it." I laughed as he gave me a look. "Seriously. It's just a follow-up. You should go back and fill out paperwork. I'm the boss and I get to make that decision."

He rolled his eyes and we headed back to my car, discussing work instead of anything important or personal. Which was good, because I was trying to come to terms with what I felt. It wasn't easy.

When we pulled into the parking lot, he didn't get out of the car right away. I looked at him.

"Go on a date with me."

My eyes widened, but I shouldn't have been

surprised. Not with what happened last night, and the tension between us.

"I thought you wanted to spend more time with your kid. Wouldn't this be a complication?"

He nodded. "You're right. But I can do both. I can find a way to make it work. There's something between us. You know that."

I swallowed hard. "I know. You're a good dad."

"And I always want to spend time with my kid. Always. But I can make time for you."

My lips twitched. "So, I'll be, what, third priority?"

His eyes went serious as he studied my face. When he pushed my hair back from my eyes, I swallowed.

"Is that a problem?"

That made me laugh, breaking some tension. Because this was likely going to be bad. But maybe it'd be okay. Maybe I wouldn't screw everything up. There *was* something there. Something I needed to see. "So, your kid first, the business that I own would be second, so I can live with third. But nothing too complicated. Nothing that hurts Lucy or the business. Or my family."

Or me.

But I didn't say that.

In answer, Hugh leaned forward and brushed his lips over mine. Anyone walking by could see us, and that would be a problem.

But I let him kiss me, and when he pulled back and pushed my hair behind my ear, he smiled.

"Okay. I'll call you."

I rolled my eyes but knew he would because he didn't lie. Not that I could tell. I needed to work though, to focus, and pretend I wasn't making a mistake. But I was. I was tired of being left behind. Tired of imagining what I could have or who I could be. Tired of everybody looking at me and their pity over getting hurt or that I had no one to come home to. And damn it, I liked him.

But dear God, the complications.

I wanted forever. Not Mr. London right now.

I went to my next job, and then the next, and it was late by the time I got home, and I already had a text from Hugh saying that I could pick the place since I knew the area, but we should make it soon. I replied, put my phone in my pocket, and went to check my mail.

I frowned at the letter inside, wondering who would write me a letter.

In handwriting I didn't recognize, it just said two words.

Miss you.

A sense of foreboding hit me hard.

I did the one thing I should do—I opened my computer and made a new file, starting a paper trail.

But I told myself this was just a joke.

Even though I didn't believe it.

Chapter Eight

Hugh

“Beware of the monster. The monster knows if you’ve eaten your vegetables. If you’ve cleaned your room. It thinks little girls may be behind on their chores.” I crept around the corner of the hallway, my bare feet padding along the tile as quietly as I could. “Come out, come out little girl. The monster’s here.”

“Never! My Teddy’s fate shall be avenged! I cleaned my room and ate my vegetables. The monster shall never win.” I put my hands over my face as Lucy pointed the Nerf gun at my head.

“No. Not that. Not the vegetables.”

"I ate all of the broccoli. Daddy saw. He needs to tell the monster I ate my vegetables."

"All of them? Are you sure." I lowered my hands and crept closer to her.

She held up the Nerf gun, her eyes narrowed. She wore a princess crown with a Marvel superhero costume. She also had on old Crocs that were probably too small for her, but it was her avenging costume.

"Did you eat all the broccoli? Or just a single piece with cheese?"

"I ate it all. And all the cheese. Because cheese is amazing!" She shot off a round before dropping the Nerf gun and running backwards and giggling.

I picked up the Nerf gun, attached it to my belt, and followed her, arms outstretched as I made an awkward growling sound.

If any of my friends back home saw this, they would've wondered what was wrong with me. But this was fine. My little girl wanted to play pretend monster superhero vegetable-eaters, so that's what we did. It was a little ridiculous, but this was the best kind of ridiculous.

"I got you," I called out, and she rushed towards me, giggling.

"No, no, no. I've got you."

And then she leapt around the corner and jumped on my back, crawling like the little spider monkey she was.

I let out a fake roar, falling to the ground in a way that kept her from getting hurt.

"I cleaned my room. I win. Always." She threw back her head and howled like a wolf and I began tickling her stomach. She kicked out, nearly getting me in the face, but I kept laughing.

"Are you sure it was all your vegetables?"

"Yes, I promise," she said, the giggles never stopping.

"Let's see. Let the monster see." I stood up, tossing her over my shoulder. She kicked out and I barely missed a knee to the nose as I carried her to the doorway. Her room was clean, her bed only a little messy since she had been crawling over it earlier. But she had put everything away, and it looked like a kid lived there. It wasn't pristine, there were no straight corners and there was probably dust because I hadn't had time to dust recently. But she had cleaned her room, just like she was supposed to. I thought we were doing this whole dad-and-daughter thing pretty well.

"Well, it seems you have passed inspection. For now." I let her feet hit the ground and kept my hand on her shoulder, giving it a squeeze. "You did a good job, baby."

"Monsters don't call me baby. I'm not a baby."

I frowned down at my daughter, wondering if I had made a misstep. I was still getting used to this whole full-time dad thing. Lucy had always been in my life, just like I had always been in hers, but that didn't mean I knew what I was doing. "I know you're not a baby, but you're always going to be my baby. I'm sorry, it's in the dad rules."

Lucy gave out such a put-upon sigh that I almost laughed.

She was so much like my family, it was a little disconcerting.

My parents loved Lucy, though they didn't get to see her often. We didn't get to travel overseas too much, not with my business or the fact that I hadn't had full custody. Now that I had full custody, I was starting over, so getting the time off would come. Yes, the Montgomerys were all about family. But it was also a job, and I couldn't ask for two weeks off right out of the gate. My family would be out soon to come visit though, because they wanted to see Lucy. But visits only went so far, and while Lucy loved her grandparents and aunt, I was more excited to see them. But first I had to figure out how to keep going as a single dad, not screw up my daughter's life, and hope to hell that her mother hadn't already done that.

Just thinking of Cheryl sent rage through my system, but I told myself I didn't need to focus on that. Cheryl wasn't the most important thing in this situation. Lucy was. I had to figure out how to be the disciplinarian, the caregiver, and the touchstone in my daughter's life. I hadn't been strong enough to keep Cheryl happy, and Cheryl decided that we didn't matter.

Just the thought angered me, but I told myself it was fine.

That's all I could do.

"What's wrong, Daddy? You look sad."

I went down to my knees, bringing Lucy in for a big hug. She wrapped her little arms around me, hugging me tight. That was my kid. The best fucking kid ever.

"I'm fine. I think I'm just tired. I didn't get a lot of sleep."

I had been dreaming about Daisy, but I wasn't going to say that out loud.

"Should we go to the park?" Lucy asked, her voice barely above a whisper in my ear. I kissed the top of her head and leaned back.

"Of course. But you're going to have to change."

She sighed dramatically. "Really? Do you not like my princess hero?"

"I love your princess hero," I said, my hand over my chest. "However, those shoes are going to fall apart any day now, and I don't want you tripping. Honestly, you probably shouldn't even be wearing them here."

She staggered back, hand over her chest as if I had just injured her. "What? No! Not my Crocs. Crocky. Crocky!" And then she dramatically flopped onto the pile of stuffed animals, and I barely resisted the urge to burst out laughing. My daughter, the drama star.

"Okay, I guess we'll let you keep Crocky, but if you trip and break a leg, that's on you. I'm not going to help."

"You wouldn't help me if I broke a leg?" she asked, blinking those wide eyes.

"Well, I would if you were wearing shoes that fit you."

"So I can get new Crockies?"

"I see," I said, narrowing my gaze. Oh, she was a grifter. I loved her. "We'll get you some new ones, because your toes don't actually fit in those."

"It's okay. I will change because I want to go play on the playground and I don't want to hurt my superhero costume."

"Okay, let's do that."

"Can I wear the crown?" she asked.

I smiled, wondering where my child got all of this guile and energy. It wasn't from me.

"Yes. You can. But be careful with it, okay?"

"Okay. I love you, Daddy." She kissed my cheek, then ran off to go change. I sighed as I re-stacked her stuffed animals. She was so darn cute. She had me wrapped around her finger, and while I wasn't sure if she knew it yet, she would figure it out soon.

I unhooked the Nerf gun from my belt, put it with

her other toys, and went to go change clothes. I was currently in my at-home sweats and a shirt that had seen better days. I hadn't changed after we woke up because Lucy wanted to play, then we had made pancakes, and continued our monster game after breakfast. It was a good day off. I had done the grocery shopping earlier in the week, and we had cleaned together. So today was just about time with my kid—which was the reason I moved here to begin with and taken the job with the Montgomerys. At my old job I probably would still be in the office, even when I wasn't supposed to be working, or at home doing paperwork. I loved my job, don't get me wrong. But Lucy needed me to be here.

I quickly changed and grabbed my phone, wallet, and keys. Lucy bounded in, wearing everything but shoes.

"So, no Crockies means no shoes at all?" I asked. Since when did I say Crockies?

"I can't find my socks."

"I folded them and put them in your drawer, baby."

"But I don't know which ones I want. I don't want to ruin my good socks."

"Let's find some then." We spent a good five minutes going through every single pair of her socks before she picked the plain white ones. I barely resisted the urge to sigh aloud. I loved my kid, I really did, but when she decided to get picky about certain things, it gave me a headache. However, I wouldn't trade any of these moments for the world.

We hopped in my SUV, after we grabbed snacks and water, because a quick trip to the park was never quick, and made our way there. She bounded out and threw her arms around a little girl I didn't recognize. I then noticed the heavily tattooed man standing beside her.

"Hey, Sebastian."

Sebastian Montgomery waved me over.

"Hey, Hugh. I didn't know you and Lucy were coming out today."

I narrowed my eyes at my daughter. "I think we've been played. Was this your daughter's idea?"

"We wanted to see each other, and we wanted you guys to be best friends."

Another man came up beside Sebastian, holding back a laugh. I lifted my chin in hello to Kane. Well, apparently it was a Montgomery afternoon, and my daughter wanted to play with her new best friend.

"Daddy, this is Nora. Nora, this is my daddy. He's from England. And he has an accent, and the teacher said it made him sound dreamy. But I wasn't supposed to hear that because I was running back to my desk to get my stuffy, so she didn't know that I heard that, so we can't tell her."

Lucy said that all in one breath, and both Sebastian and Kane burst out laughing.

"Dreamy?" Kane asked, and I nearly flipped him off before I remembered where we were.

"Shush, Montgomery."

"I'm not a Montgomery," Kane sing-songed.

"Yes, you are. You're my uncle, so you're a Montgomery. Because I have all the Montgomerys." Nora put her hands on her hips and glared at her uncle. Or maybe it was her second cousin. I really didn't know, but the Montgomerys went by aunt and uncle to the younger generation, so I went with that.

"Lucy, baby, the next time you want to come play with your friend, just tell me. You don't need to make up an elaborate scenario so I will take you to the park."

Lucy ran and threw herself into my arms, and I huffed out a breath as she knocked the wind out of me. My kid was strong.

"Sorry, Daddy. I just wanted to see Nora, and I wanted you to see her daddy, and then she brought her Uncle Kane, and everything is great. I love you. Can I go play on the swing set?"

"Let's walk over there together, since I don't actually know how the swing set works."

"You know how the swings work."

"But I don't know these swings. Let's check them out together."

She rolled her eyes dramatically as Nora took her hand and they ran towards the swings.

"Well, Nora's great at making friends, and already has two best friends, and it looks like she's trying to add a third."

"I was really worried about moving Lucy to a new area, a new school and all that. I'm glad she's making friends."

"Nora's had the same two best friends since she was a baby, and they were all hanging out in daycare together. But she's great at making friends, and since she knows you work with the Montgomerys, you've sort of been adopted in." Sebastian winced as Kane laughed beside him.

"It seems easy to get adopted into this family," I mumbled, and Kane laughed again.

"Well, we do our best to make it difficult to get out. Remind us to tell you about the cult."

I nearly tripped over my feet as I watched Nora and Lucy play.

"Cult?" I asked, worried.

Sebastian scowled at Kane. "It's a family joke—we're not actually a cult. Stop scaring the guy. I know you like working with him, you don't want him to quit and run away and take his kid with him. Then I'd have to deal with Nora being sad. Do you really want your niece sad?"

Kane winced. "Sorry. It's just a joke, because there's so many of us. I promise we're not actually a cult. We just like cheese."

Confused, I turned away from them, looking at my daughter and her new friend. "I'm glad she's making friends."

"I don't know the whole story, but if you ever want to talk about why you're here, rather than living back in England with that *dreamy* accent of yours, we can go get a beer and talk."

I snorted at that. "I don't think her teacher would be happy to know that Lucy overheard that. Her teacher's actually very nice, and very married to her wife."

Kane laughed. "It's the accent. Gets them every time. Not me though. I can refuse."

I believed him, and yet there was an odd sadness in his gaze. Maybe I was seeing things, or maybe there was something more to what he just said. These Montgomerys were killing me.

"Come on, let's go sit over here and watch the girls play. They're old enough now that they don't need us to push them on the swings."

I reached out and squeezed Sebastian's shoulder. "It's okay. You can be sad about that. I sure as hell am."

"Seriously, she was just a baby a minute ago. I don't understand how they grow up so quick."

"I don't get it. I don't like it."

"Man, being a dad sounds a little depressing," Kane said as he came and sat next to us on the bench, watching the girls play.

"It can be fun, it is fun. It's the best fucking thing I've ever done in my life," Sebastian said confidently.

"Same here. And the hardest thing I've ever done. I wasn't always allowed to be in her life every minute. I didn't have full custody until recently." I explained how I had gotten full custody, because keeping secrets like that wasn't going to help anyone. They needed to know while Lucy's trust in me might not be fragile, her trust in everyone else could break in an instant.

"Is Lucy doing okay?"

"We have a therapist. It's the best thing I could think of. I don't know what to do. She doesn't ask about Cheryl much. She just fell into this, because it's a big move. All big changes. But one day she's going to figure out that her mom's not coming back. By choice." I growled that, because I knew Nora lost her mother during childbirth, and Sebastian had been the one to pick up the pieces. A completely different situation, and one that I knew they would heal from, but never be fully whole. Because that's what life did, broke you into a thousand pieces and sometimes you could put yourself together, but you were never the same. And maybe you shouldn't be.

We talked about lighter things until Lucy and Nora came running up for water and snacks.

"Hey, Daddy, are we going to eat dinner with Daisy again?" she asked quickly.

I froze as both Kane and Sebastian swung their heads to me.

Well, I could do my best to keep secrets and keep my relationship—whatever that may be with Daisy—secret, but children always knew. And they can never keep secrets.

"Maybe. But remember, she just happened to be in the same restaurant as us, and we invited her to have dinner with us."

"Well, she's very pretty. I think you should see her again. I like her." She handed me her water bottle and her half-empty bag of fruit snacks, and ran back to play with Nora.

"So...I have questions," Kane said quickly.

"We both have questions," Sebastian added.

I groaned and leaned back, keeping my mouth shut.

I didn't have answers. Especially not when I had a date tomorrow with her.

I had a feeling this was a mistake waiting to happen.

Chapter Nine

Hugh

"I am glad we get to see Daisy again. Isn't she the best? I love her. I mean, I don't know her, but I feel like I love her. She's just so great. And nice. And Nora says she is the best babysitter. Of course, she says that about all of her aunts and uncles because they really love her. I'm so happy she has so many people that love her. I know you love me. And Grandma and Grandpa love me, and auntie loves me. But Nora has so many people that love her. Isn't that just the best?" Lucy barely breathed through that entire ramble, and with each passing word, I went from a slight panic to a brutal heartache. It was like she stabbed me over and over again. It was partially my fault and I was going to have to fix it somehow.

I was already dressed for my date, in dark slacks and a Henley shirt. We were just going out to dinner, something we could pass off as a work meeting if we needed to lie. But there had been enough lying. Especially since Lucy had brought up Daisy the day before, and I could only imagine what Kane and Sebastian had said to the rest of the family, or to Daisy directly.

But, while Daisy was important to this conversation, and something I would need to discuss more with Lucy, that wasn't what was hurting her.

I cupped her chin. "Lucy. I love you. Your grandma and grandpa love you. So does your aunt. We're your family. They may be far away, but they're only a phone call away. They don't mind even if you accidentally call them when it's one in the morning there." She smiled, though it didn't reach her eyes. That had been a video phone call nobody had been expecting, they answered in a panic, and I rushed into the room wondering why I heard shouting. I realized it was because they were worried something had happened. Not because Lucy wanted to show them her loose tooth.

We smiled and laughed at it, and we learned rules about using the phone. But they would always answer. Because my parents loved their granddaughter.

But they weren't her mom. And neither was I.

"I know they love me. You love me too. I just get jealous. I know it's wrong to be jealous. Because I have to be happy with what I have, and I am. I love you but I also want all the things."

Lucy's babysitter was on her way over, someone Sebastian introduced us to, so I had a few minutes with my baby girl.

"Okay, Lucy. Let's talk."

"I don't want to make you sad. I'm not sad." She did that thing where she spoke quickly enough to maybe mask her own feelings from herself and me. But I was learning. We were both learning together. I sat on the ground cross-legged and brought her into my arms. She snuggled into me, but she didn't cry. She just sounded sad. That little sigh broke my heart.

"Why didn't Mommy love me?"

I took a deep breath, knowing I didn't have an answer. I practiced this a thousand times. Had even spoken to Lucy about it numerous times. And yet there was nothing. And I hated it.

What did you say to a little girl who you love more than the stars themselves when there were no words to make it better?

"Your mom needed to make decisions for herself, decisions that we don't understand. But we talked about it, remember? We said that there was enough love in the world between just the two of us that we could handle everything." These weren't the right words. I knew they weren't. And I knew I'd be calling the family therapist again in the morning. I was making mistake after mistake with my kid. I was never going to forgive Cheryl for that.

"I know she wanted to be with her new family. The one without me. But why wasn't I good enough? I cleaned my room. I tried to be good. Why did she go away?"

I hugged her tight. I didn't have any answers. There wasn't anything I could do to make this better for my baby girl. But I needed to figure something out.

"I don't know why your mommy had to go away. I don't have the answers for her choices. But no matter what, know that I love you. I am never leaving. I will always be here for you. I know I'm not your mommy, but I am your daddy. I love you. We are going to figure out this new life of ours together. We're a team. You're going to have to help me, too." She pulled away, wide-eyed. I wiped the tears from her cheeks, rage warring with the ache inside me. But I couldn't lean into the anger, that wouldn't help anything.

"You need help from me?" she asked.

"Yes, because I'm learning how to do this too. And you know we're a team. That means I need you to tell me when you're not feeling good. When you're feeling sad. I need you to tell me things. Like you're doing right now. And I might not always have answers—I wish I did—but we can figure them out together. Because, no matter what, I'm going to be here."

Lucy leaned forward and patted my cheek. I loved this little girl with all of my heart.

Who could ever leave her?

"I love you. And I'll tell you when I'm sad. But will you tell me when you're sad?"

I smiled and did my best to put on the brave face my daughter needed. "I'll try my best."

"Okay. I love you." She snuggled into me, and I knew what I had to do next.

I pulled my phone out of my pants pocket, adjusting Lucy on my lap as I did, and texted the babysitter. I offered to pay them, to say I was sorry for canceling at the last minute, but they didn't mind and told me to enjoy my night with my daughter. There were some good people in the world, and I had to remember that. Even if, between my job and Lucy's mom, it didn't feel like it.

And then knowing this was best, I texted the next person.

Me: *Lucy is having a tough night without her mom. I'm going to have to cancel. I'm sorry.*

Daisy: *I understand completely. More than you know. Hug her tight, okay? And tell her I'm thinking about her. If that'll help.*

I remembered that yes, she did understand. It wasn't

the exact same situation, but it was close enough that I wondered how Daisy survived not having a mom in her life either. Then again, she had her stepmom. The woman that eventually adopted her.

Me: *Thank you. Seriously. Tough night figuring things out.*

Daisy: *I understand. I promise.*

I set the phone down and leaned against the wall, listening as Lucy talked about her favorite TV show. I just held my kid, wondering what the hell I was going to do next.

Dating didn't seem to be in the cards, and that was fine. Lucy had to come first. Always.

We sat on the ground for a good thirty minutes before Lucy was laughing again, and we had just started figuring out what we were going to order for dinner when the doorbell rang. Lucy ran to the door.

"Let me see who it is."

"You know the rules," I ordered, alarm sliding up my spine. With my job, I got to see the worst side of things. So no, my elementary-school-age kid wouldn't be opening the door on her own.

I looked through the peephole, and a smile spread over my face.

"Well, Lucy, I guess we don't have to figure out what we're doing for dinner."

I opened the door for Daisy, who was bouncing from foot to foot, looking nervous.

"Hi. I totally thought this was a good idea at the time, and I'm afraid I have stepped in it."

"Daisy! You're here!" Lucy ran and threw her arms around Daisy's legs. Daisy wobbled for a bit, since both hands were full of food, and I leaned forward and took the food from her.

"You okay?"

"Oh, I'm fine."

"You're here, you're here. And you brought our favorite food. See, Daddy? She brought Indian food. Isn't Daisy the best?"

Tears long forgotten, she tugged on Daisy's hand and pulled her inside.

"Lucy seems happy to see you."

Daisy met my gaze, and I saw the worry there. "And you? I can leave the food and go. I know you guys need some time together. I just thought you might want some food, since you planned on eating out."

I just met her gaze. "Go follow Lucy into the living room. We're figuring out what to watch. I guess you can have a say."

I wanted to kiss her, but doing so in front of Lucy might be an issue. I hadn't dated at all since I became a dad, so we were going to navigate these waters slowly.

"So, what did you get? Oh do you want to help me set the table? Daddy likes when I help set the table. But I'm too short to reach the plates."

"I can help. You just show me where to go. I've never been here before."

"Okay, over here," Lucy said as she bounced towards the little kitchen. "The plates are up there. I have a stool, but I'm not allowed to get the plates myself."

"Tell her why." I raised a brow at my daughter, who blushed.

"Because I broke one. I didn't mean to, but then I said a bad word."

Daisy looked at me, her eyes filled with laughter. "Now, where did she learn that?"

"School is rough these days."

"Daddy taught me. He didn't mean to. But I sometimes say it the British way like Daddy does, and then I get in even more trouble because that means I'm saying the really bad words."

"You're right. When you say the bad words the British way, they are the worst kind of words. But you should try to say the fun words instead, like queue, or cuppa, or cheeky."

I rolled my eyes at them but smiled.

"Now that you're done mocking me and my accent, let's see what you brought us."

"I'm not mocking you. Much." Daisy winked at me and gestured towards the food.

"I might've gone a little overboard. I got the butter chicken, chicken korma, and a couple other things on my favorites list, so you'll have leftovers for days. Plus two kinds of samosas, and three kinds of naan. I was hungry."

Lucy clapped her hands as she bounced around, full of energy, no sign that she was crying earlier. That was my kid, resilient as hell. I was so lucky she felt safe enough to tell me what she felt.

I wasn't sure what I would do if she ever stopped doing that. Nor was I sure what I was going to do when she hit the preteen and teen years. I held back a shudder. Oh, I was not prepared for that. I was not even prepared for this pseudo-date where my daughter bounced between us.

I met Daisy's gaze. "Thank you. Seriously." I reached out and squeezed her hand, and Daisy squeezed right back.

"You're welcome. Let's start eating because I'm starving."

"Same here. I'm starving," Lucy replied with a British accent.

I snorted as we huddled around the table. I plated Lucy's food first before getting my own.

"So, you work with Daddy? Do you keep bad guys away?"

I winced but Daisy didn't seem to mind the topic of conversation.

"I do work with your dad. And I do my best to keep the

bad guys away. Sometimes my job is just setting up cameras or talking to people so they know how to keep themselves safe. Do you know a few ways to keep yourself safe?"

"Not to talk to strangers, but if somebody asks me to see a puppy or if I want candy, to scream and try to go to an adult I know or an adult in charge." She continued to list off a few things I had taught her over the years. Daisy nodded along and added a few things of her own.

"And when you get older, I can help you with self-defense."

"I think I can help her with that," I said, narrowing my gaze at her.

"Well, you are built like a brick house which, don't get me wrong, is nice, but you're going to be a lot taller than Lucy. I could help with her lower center of gravity."

"You should both help me. I like it when you work together." Lucy looked between us, and a small alarm went off in me, but I figured it was nothing. My daughter only liked Daisy as a friend.

Which was far different than how I felt about Daisy. Not that I was going to let myself think about that.

We cleaned up after dinner, then went to the living room to watch a Disney movie. Lucy sank between us on the couch and asked if we could both cuddle with her, so that meant my arm was around Daisy's shoulders, and Lucy was snuggled between the two of us.

I looked over to see if Daisy minded at all, but she was laughing at something that my daughter said as they watched the movie, and I forced myself to relax. This was fine. Not quite a date, but maybe it was. Lucy fell asleep halfway through the movie, so I paused the stream and quietly cleared my throat.

"She sleeps like the dead. Seriously, nothing's going to wake her unless she wants to wake up."

"I'll start cleaning up in here," Daisy said, gesturing to the snacks we had brought out. I was unsure how Lucy packed away so much, but she was growing, a growth spurt hitting her hard.

"I'm just going to tuck her in," I whispered.

Daisy smiled and I sat up, Lucy in my arms. She wasn't a baby anymore; she was getting bigger every day, but I could still hold her for now. I never wanted to let go. We were skipping brushing her teeth and getting her in her pajamas tonight, but she was in loungewear with no buttons or zippers or anything, so it was fine. One night of missing brushing her teeth wouldn't hurt. At least I hoped not.

Lucy began snoring, and I smiled as I tucked her in, made sure the monitor was on, and closed the door behind me.

When I went back out to the living room, Daisy was frowning at something on her phone.

"Everything okay?" I asked as I sat next to her on the couch.

"Oh, it's fine. Just that other security firm being an asshole."

I raised a brow. "Seriously?"

"Now that they can't buy us out, they want us out. They're putting in rival bids for nearly everything we're doing. It's annoying as hell." She paused and looked like she wanted to say something else.

When she didn't, I leaned forward and asked, "What is it?"

"Nothing. Tonight was nice. I know it isn't exactly what we planned, and I sort of just barged in. Thank you for letting me stay."

I pushed her hair back from her face, my thumb brushing her cheek.

"You made my kid's night. I'm sorry for canceling, but thank you for coming over anyway."

"I'm really not good at this, you know."

"Good at what?"

"Dating, figuring out what I want. You know this is wrong, right? You know this is only going to end badly?"

I nodded, my gut rolling. "Maybe. Probably. But as long as Lucy doesn't get hurt, that's what I care about most." I said, knowing we were both lying to ourselves.

I leaned forward and brushed my lips against hers. I deepened the kiss when she moaned, and then I was leaning over her, pressing her back into the couch. I slid my hands up her sides to cup her breasts and she moaned. I hadn't made out on a couch since I was a teenager, but it was the hottest thing I'd ever done. I was somehow between her legs, rubbing myself against her as we kissed leisurely, our hands moving over each other's bodies. The sound of panting began to fill the room, and I cursed, leaning back. I pressed my forehead against hers, trying to catch my breath as she smiled up at me.

"We are making out like teenagers."

I kissed her again, just a quick one, because I could.

"My daughter sleeps hard, but let's not test that."

Daisy nodded and we both sat up, adjusting our clothes.

"You're right. I don't want to have to have that conversation." We both shuddered. "I should be heading home anyway. We have work in the morning."

I winced. "Lucy has a day off school for a teacher workday. I'll be dropping her off at the Montgomery Daycare Center."

"It's where I went often."

"At least the Colorado Springs satellite version?" I asked with a laugh.

"Pretty much. Our families wanted to make sure that we had a safe space."

"I'll see you at work tomorrow." I paused. "By the

way, Daisy, Lucy sort of brought you up in front of Sebastian and Kane at the park. I didn't know we were meeting them there, but my child is diabolical."

Daisy's eyes filled with laughter. "Oh, I know. They both texted me. I don't know if the entire grapevine knows, yet, but there will be no more hiding what happened. I mean, we don't have to tell them about the wedding per se, but I'm pretty sure they know something. And the fact that I haven't been called into detention means that it's okay."

I winced. "This is complicated, Daisy."

She nodded. "You're right. Probably too complicated."

I should stop this now. It'd be best for both of us. But I couldn't. So, I leaned down and kissed her again, both of us relaxing at the touch.

"I'll see you at work?"

"Deal. And we'll figure it out. Somehow."

I kissed her again, and then watched as she got in her car and drove off.

This was a mistake. But it was one I knew I had to make.

Chapter Ten

DAISY

"I'm as big as a house and I love it." Lake Montgomery beamed as she leaned back in her throne, also known as the reclining chair in her living room, and rested her hands on her bulging belly. Her swollen ankles were up on the footrest, and she had on a tiara with fuzzy pompoms glued on top. She looked absolutely ridiculous and glorious.

Lake's mom snorted. "You're not quite as big as a house, darling," Arden Montgomery said with a wink. She sat down on the side throne, also known as the other reclining chair. All of Lake's aunts on her father's side of the family, the Crosses, laughed and told war stories of their pregnancies and how big they were.

A Montgomery baby shower was a force to be reckoned with. We hadn't had many in our generation yet, but with the number of people falling in love, it was going to start happening more often. Lake's cousins on her other side of the family were also procreating, and my cousins on my dad's side of the family were working on it, too.

We weren't all Montgomerys, even if it felt like it.

"I can't believe you didn't make Nick come to this," I teased as I sipped my sparkling cider.

"Yes, because I can totally see my husband at a baby shower with cucumber sandwiches, fluffy cakes, and birth stories." Lake rolled her eyes and took a bite of her cucumber sandwich. "Of course, that's completely sexist of me, all the men were invited."

"And yet they're not here," I said with a laugh.

"Of course, they aren't. They're off at that ax-throwing place, doing research to open up one of their own places while being manly men and talking about their feelings." Brooke rolled her eyes as she sat down on the couch next to me.

"Really? That doesn't sound like them." I paused. "Okay. It sounds partially like them. But I thought they were more enlightened than that."

"They are. Sometimes. And sometimes they revert.

We let them, because then they give foot rubs and then we pretend we are dainty women that need a man to help us."

Raven laughed from my other side. "Please, let me be there when we tell Sebastian I'm dainty and helpless."

I laughed, shaking my head. "You know I don't really see that happening."

"You think you have it bad, I have two of them. Oh, they're enlightened and totally know I can handle myself, but if I want to carry a heavy box into the house? Dear God, it's the worst thing ever."

"As I have two husbands just like you're about to, I feel for you," my Aunt Maya said to Greer with a laugh. "And it doesn't get any easier. They just want to make sure the little lady is safe."

"I don't know how you do it, Greer. I mean, watching Lake handle Nick? That's fun. Brooke with Leif? Amazing. Raven making sure Sebastian knows his place? Enlightening. But I couldn't handle two."

"Because anyone handling you would need to be made of strong stuff. And you don't need two—you'd get annoyed. Somehow I don't, and I don't know how." Greer shrugged and ate a bit of her canapé.

"Is it because I'm a jerk? Am I a bitch?" I asked and then winced. "Sorry, Mom. Didn't mean to curse."

My mom waved me off. "You're in a room full of Montgomerys. Cursing and cheese are sort of expected."

Lake sighed longingly. "I miss soft cheeses. And salmon. I was craving sushi the other day. Maybe that's going to be my push present. Or push gift, is that what it's called?"

"Should I mention that, back in my day, we didn't have push presents?" Aunt Maya said.

"Back in the stone ages?" Maya's daughter, Skylar, asked, before Maya narrowed her gaze at her daughter and began to chase her around the house. It didn't matter that Skylar was a full-grown adult, just like the rest of us. There had to be at least forty of us in this house. But because this was Lake's house, there was enough space for all of us, and then some.

Not only did she own part of Montgomery Ink Legacy, she also had a share in many businesses and helped others start their own small businesses. I knew that if we had needed help for Montgomery Security, she would've stepped in.

Everyone talked, laughing about their pregnancy and birth stories, but Lake's eyes got a little wider with each one.

"Okay, now you're scaring me."

"Don't be scared," her mom said as she squeezed her hand. "Never be scared. I've been there for all the years after you turned ten. All the preteens and teens and the terrible, terrible twenties, and I will be here for this too."

Lake growled. “I am just barely out of my twenties, thank you very much.”

“So instead of terrible twos it’s terrible twenties?” I asked.

“Yes, my child, tell me about it,” Mom said with a roll of her eyes, and the talk of how terrible and yet amazing we all were as kids kept going.

Raven nudged me and handed me a cupcake.

“You okay?” she asked, and I nodded.

“I am. What about you? I know we’re not being very delicate about talking about childbirth around you.”

Nora’s mother Marley had died at nineteen, during childbirth, a little over five years ago. She had been Sebastian’s first love, childhood sweetheart, and his soon-to-be wife. It didn’t even seem possible. That in this day and age that could happen, but it had. She went into cardiac arrest, and we lost her. Sebastian had been a single father for the first five years, until Raven came back to town. Raven had been Sebastian and Marley’s friend, so Raven lost her best friend, too.

This baby shower was a time of joy, but we also reflected on what we had lost. And I was grateful that I was born into a family like this. Okay, perhaps I had been adopted later, much like Lake, but my father had always been there for me. And my aunts. The ones that weren’t the Montgomerys. I was blessed to have this family. I would never forget that.

"Okay, time for the next game," Brooke said as she looked down at her notes. Brooke had organized this entire thing, and I wasn't sure how she had been able to do that. She was a physics professor and researcher, a brilliant woman, and a mom to two kids. But Lake and Brooke were practically sisters, and she wanted to do this for Lake.

"I'm a little afraid," I said, and Raven shuddered.

"I'm not going to tell you about the games at my friend's baby shower. There were tastings of *things*." She shivered.

I frowned. "Like baby food?"

"No, worse," Greer said.

"Okay, now I'm worried."

Aria came and sat on the floor in front of me and handed me another cupcake. I was going to get a sugar high.

"Oh, please don't discuss that. I heard about that. It was all food, but it didn't look like food when they forced you to take a bite."

"Please do not share more details," Lake said, her hand on her stomach. "I'm nauseous now."

"Well, I'm nauseous too."

Raven tapped Aria on the head and scowled.

"Just because you are my fiancé's twin sister doesn't mean I won't slap you upside the head."

"I think that actually gives you permission." Aria winked at me, and I shoved her shoulder.

"Be nice. I love that you have a new job that you're so amazing at, but I wish you worked for us so I could keep you in line."

Aria rolled her eyes. "Like you could ever keep me in line."

Aria and Sebastian's mother cleared her throat. "This is true. Nobody can. Maybe Sebastian."

"Sorry, he's too busy with Nora and me now. Aria is going to have to figure out how to be kept in line on her own."

Aria and Raven glared at each other before they burst out laughing.

We were all growing up. Somehow my cousins were getting married and having babies and we were the adults in the room. Our parents would always be there for us, but there were children like Nora and Luke and Landon who needed us. We weren't the kids anymore. I knew that. Of course I knew that, but I was still trying to figure out what I was doing and how I could make it in this big bad world.

Thankfully we finished a quick game of baby names, and then it was time for presents.

I had gotten something right off the registry, because I had no idea what to get for a baby. But there were books and onesies, and that was what Auntie Daisy could do.

Because we had such a big family, we were only allowed to get certain things from the registry, and everything else either went to charity, or to the daycare center.

After the gifts were opened, I mingled around a bit, and tried not to think about how Lucy felt. Little Lucy, who had been born into a family that wasn't like mine. While I knew I was blessed, her story felt too familiar.

I had no idea where my mom even lived. If she had ever loved me. Was that what Lucy felt? I knew Hugh was doing his best, just like my dad had, but I'd still felt the lack. I hadn't let myself think about it, but it had been there. What about Lucy?

"Baby, what's wrong?" I looked up to see my mother standing there, a curious look in Adrienne Montgomery-Knight's eyes.

"I'm just thinking. It's a beautiful baby shower."

My mom brushed my hair from my face, concern etched in her features.

"I can tell that's not everything, what's wrong, baby?" she asked again.

"I'm just thinking about my mom. Well, the other one. Because you're my mom. I love you." I closed my eyes and sighed. "I'm not saying this right."

My mom cupped my face, like she always had ever since I was a little girl.

"I've always done my best never to say how I feel about *that woman* in front of you."

My eyes widened at her tone when she said "that woman." But my mom was correct. She had never said an unkind word about my birth mother.

"Really?" I asked, curious.

"I will never forgive her for what she did. But the anger that was within me? Now it's just pity. Because you are glorious. You are brilliant and strong and I am blessed that I get to be your mother. No matter what you do in the future, I'm going to be proud. Because you are a good person. And she never got to see that. She walked away and I can't hate her for it because I got to have you. So that's the selfish part of me. But also, fuck her. Because I get you and your dad and your siblings. And honestly, we're better off. I'll never forgive her for hurting you, but that pity? It soothes the numb."

I hadn't realized I was crying until she wiped a tear from my cheek. I looked into my mom's eyes, surprised again that we were the same height. But I was still her little girl.

"I still hate her sometimes. And then I don't think about her. Someone asks me my mom's name and you are the first person that comes to mind, because of course you're my mom. Why wouldn't that be the case? I forget that you weren't there when I was born. I forget that you weren't pregnant with me. I forget that Amy was your first pregnancy. Isn't that weird?"

My mom shook her head. "I forget too. And I think that is because we were meant for each other. Just like I was meant for your dad and for Amy. I love you. And we are one example of how families can be made. I mean, what does 'traditional family' mean anyway?"

"You're a tattoo artist who is married to another tattoo artist, and you guys fight over who can ink your kids' skin. I'm pretty sure nothing about us is traditional."

"That is true." She squeezed my hand. "Do you want to tell me where this came from?"

I looked around at our family as they laughed and talked as the baby shower wound down.

"It's not just this. I met someone."

My mom squeezed my hand tight.

"Is it that man that you work with?"

My gaze shot to hers and she held up her free hand. "I swear, this family is better than any gossip train out there."

I laughed, I couldn't help it.

"Yes. It's Hugh. And he's a single dad too." I explained a little bit about Lucy's situation. My mom's eyes darkened.

"That bitch."

I smiled, righteous in my own anger. "Agreed. I guess it just hit a little too close to home."

"And it makes things super-complicated no matter what. Because you're just in the first sparks of this relationship."

"And we work together. And he's not my best friend, like you were with Dad. And no, I don't want any of the details," I added quickly.

My mom laughed. "No. Those are mine. Just be safe. Be careful. Be who you are. You're a good person, Daisy, and Lucy's lucky to have you, no matter who you are in her life."

I hugged my mother tightly and relaxed. I didn't know what would happen next, what would happen with Hugh.

But I wouldn't hurt Lucy. Just like my mom Adrienne hadn't hurt me.

I could at least take comfort in that.

Chapter Eleven

HUGH

"Seriously, all he did was stare at me while I put up the camera, as if he thought I had no idea what I was doing, or if I was supposed to magically get it up there without getting on a ladder."

I snorted, setting my beer down. "Was it because he wanted to watch you get up the ladder? Or he wanted to do it himself?"

Daisy sat back in her chair and pushed her hair back from her face. And it was such a great face. It was hard for me to stay focused on it though, and not let my gaze go down the long line of her neck to her bare shoulders. It still seemed a bit surreal to me that she was right there in front of me, and we were on a date. A date.

Was this our first? Our third? Did a single dance at a wedding and then a night that I could still remember every taste and sound of count as a date? Did our impromptu dinner at the Indian restaurant with my daughter count? Did takeout at my house count? I didn't know. I had never done this before. Not with Lucy as such a large part of my life. I had always wanted her to be the constant part of my life, and I had never been able to have that. And now that I did, I was so afraid of ruining it, I didn't know if what I was doing right now was the right thing, or one of the most selfish things I had ever done. It was probably the latter.

"I was pretty sure it was a little bit of both," Daisy answered, pulling me out of my thoughts. She wore a strapless top over long pants. It almost looked like some sort of jumpsuit, though I wasn't into fashion so I had no idea if that was the case or not. She had her hair down, falling in waves down her back. She was honestly one of the most gorgeous women I had ever met. I was so damn lucky that she was across from me. Especially considering the fact that while she technically wasn't my boss, she still was up there in the hierarchy and we worked together.

"Now what are you worried about?" she asked, and I shook my head, reminding myself that I needed to stay present—something I wasn't very good at.

"Just wondering if this is such a good idea." I wasn't

sure I should have been that honest about it, but as she smiled at me, that same worry in her gaze, I figured it was good to put it right out in the open. We were both thinking it, we might as well worry about it together.

"Honestly, yes. This is probably a mistake. But if we're going to call it that, we made that at the wedding. Though if we stick with our plan and keep things separate, it won't be a problem. Right?"

I reached across the table and squeezed her hand. "We can live in denial, that is perfectly fine."

"That's what I like about you, Hugh. You're good at the whole denial thing."

I shook my head and sat back, missing her touch already. "No. I'm really not. But I don't mind lying to myself right now."

"Well, at least we're both good at that."

"Anyway, what did you do to the man?"

Daisy frowned. "The man?" Then she snapped her fingers, her eyes brightening. "Oh yes. The client. Well, I continued to work, but as I went up the ladder, the man seemed to come to a decision and proceeded to reach up and grab my ass so I 'wouldn't fall off the ladder.' Even though I hadn't faltered."

An unfamiliar rage settled through me. "Does this man still live? Does he have all his limbs?"

Daisy winked and sipped her sparkling wine.

"He lives. And I didn't even bruise him."

"You know, that surprises me. Honestly. Not that you're violent," I added quickly, as her eyes narrowed. "You stand up for yourself. Something I'm trying to ensure Lucy can do too."

Daisy grinned, her whole face brightening. She looked even more beautiful, something I hadn't thought possible. And that was a problem because I was already a goner. Damn it.

"It's not like that. I politely requested that he remove his hands from my ass, or he was going to feel it later. Not my ass," she added quickly, before laughing. "I meant I was going to kick his ass and make sure that when he found his nuts, he would never be able to use them again. I even explained it using polite words."

I was lucky I wasn't taking a drink when she said that, because I burst out laughing, drawing the attention of a few people around us.

"You know, that's what I like about you."

"Because I'm dainty and I never say a bad word?"

"Sure. We'll go with that."

Daisy shrugged. "My mom's worse. But she did teach my sister and me to stand up for ourselves. My father, too."

"Did you fire him? The client," I clarified.

Daisy shook her head. "Not then. We should have, in retrospect."

I leaned forward. "What do you mean, in retrospect?"

She sighed. "Because he hit on Jennifer, and then me again. Cornered us at an event. It got weird. And then he tried to sue us when his building exploded. It didn't matter that I was almost inside when it happened and got injured from it."

"The man who hit on you and put his hands on you owned the building that exploded?"

Daisy nodded. "Yes. And then tried to sue our company because he thought we did it. Even though we were just doing our first reconnaissance. Our notes and tapes confirmed that. He didn't have a chance to win his case. But he tried to drag our name through the mud, as did Sherman Priority Security." She said the words with such a snarl, that I narrowed my eyes.

"The place that keeps trying to underbid us?"

"Yep. They do shoddy work, they try to steal our people, and they try to steal our clients. So when Mr. Grabby Hands decided he was going to ruin us because we happened to be near the building when it exploded and I got hurt, Sherman Priority took him on. It's ridiculous. We're in Denver fucking Colorado." She winced and looked around, but no one seemed to be paying attention. "Sorry for cursing."

"I think I curse more than you, you're fine. Let's try not to do that in front of Lucy because she can't curse at school. It's a whole thing, and then I have to deal with other parents."

Daisy laughed. "Oh, I get it. Especially because the Montgomerys have the worst language ever."

"It's a sign of character. There have been studies."

"I know. The whole family have those studies bookmarked in case we need to fight the good fight."

"But seriously, the city is huge. There's more than enough space for our two companies. There *are* more than our two. I just don't think they like that we're family oriented and they can't break us."

"But they still try to steal your people."

"Not all of our team are Montgomerys. You aren't."

"That is true. And you don't have many full-time staff, mostly contractors."

"We only need them for large events. We have the ability to cover their insurance if possible; it's a whole complicated process that Noah deals with and I don't have to." Daisy beamed as she said it, and I laughed.

"As someone who used to own a business, I'm with you there. I'm glad Noah is smart enough to handle it."

"Plus, our new hire, Kate? She's brilliant. Noah can actually spend time with Ford and Greer now, and not spend so much time on the books."

"That's good." I paused. "I should probably mention the security company that shall not be named has tried to poach me more than once. In fact, they called today."

Daisy scowled, and for some reason it made her look even hotter. This was an issue. "What? What did they say? What did they offer you? You better not have taken it."

I held up my hands and shook my head. "First off, I wouldn't do that. I made a promise and I like you guys. I don't like the idea of working for a company that would try to underbid and steal employees. And while it might make things easier if you and I weren't working together, I'd rather deal with the potential fallout of that than work for your arch-nemesis."

"You and I have nothing to do with it," she said, before she sighed. "Okay, that's a complete lie. I would hate you if you worked for them. And while it would make more sense because I wouldn't be anywhere near being your boss, you would work for the people I hate. I just can't believe they did that."

"They did. And they suck. But I'm not working for them. I'm working for you. Even if it makes things complicated."

"I think I like things complicated," she said with a laugh, and then her eyes widened before a huge smile spread on her face.

Only she was looking over my shoulder, not at me. I turned and saw a big man with tattoos running down his arms, wide shoulders, and a big beard. I hoped it was one of her numerous family members.

But based on the way he looked at her? No. Definitely not family.

And then I realized exactly who this man was. He wasn't wearing a tux like he had the night I'd met him at the wedding, but that glower was familiar.

I held back my scowl as Daisy stood up and wrapped her arms around the very large man.

"Hey there, Daisy. I didn't know you'd be out tonight." The damn man hugged her tightly, and then kept his hand on her hip as he looked at me.

Though he was probably my height, he was broader, with a fighter's build. I hated him on sight. I hated that he still had his hand on her hip even though she had let hers drop.

She looked between us and rolled her eyes, stepping away from him and letting his hand fall.

"Crew, this is Hugh. Hugh, this is Crew. Crew's one of my best friends. And he helps me train." Daisy took her seat across from me, so I took that as a win, until she opened her mouth to say, "He's also my ex, but it's not like that. Crew, if you could stop acting like a jealous ex—which you've never done before in your life—that would be great."

"What? Just looking out for you."

"I have forty-seven male cousins and even more female cousins to do that for me. I don't need you for that."

Her voice was crisp as she spoke, and I barely held back a smirk.

She was standing up for me. Okay, she was standing up for herself, but I was going to pretend it was for me as well.

"It's nice to meet you," I said, putting a little more posh in my accent than I normally had.

From the roll of Daisy's eyes and Crew's smirk, they both understood what I was doing. But what the hell, women loved the accent, and I was going to use it to my advantage.

"I see we're out on a work date. Enjoying yourself?"

"Crew, don't start."

"The rest of them know you're out here?"

"If you don't shut up, I'm going to kick your ass, and you showed me all the moves to take you down."

"I'm sure I have a few too," I added nonchalantly, but Daisy just shook her head at me.

Now what did that mean?

"Fine, I'm meeting a friend for a drink. But it was good to meet you. At least to lay eyes on you. You know, just so you know where we stand."

"Oh, I think I know exactly where we stand," I said.

"Boys. Let's not. We all know that I can take you both out."

"That is true. But I don't mind it." I winked at Daisy, who just smiled, and Crew laughed.

"Have fun. And don't worry. I'm the easy one to get through." Crew smirked and headed to the bar, where a woman with a low-cut dress and long blond hair waited.

She pouted at him, until Cruz slid his thumb along her cheek and she let out a soft giggle.

I turned to Daisy, who shrugged.

"He doesn't usually act like the growly ex. I'm sorry about that. Do you want to head out? We finished dessert."

I sipped the rest of my drink, giving me a second to gather my thoughts. "Your cousin Leif and his wife Brooke have Lucy for a sleepover with her new best friend. So I have all night. I didn't get to finish my dessert."

There was an edge of jealousy in my voice.

"Hugh, is this going to be a problem?"

"No, it's not." I stood and held out my hand. When she slid her hand into mine, it was all I could do not to look over at Crew to show him I won. That she was mine. If only for the night.

I lifted her up, my hands on her thighs, her back pressed against the door.

"Hugh."

"That's it, say my name. Tell me exactly who you're with right now."

"I don't like this jealous side of you."

"I don't either. So let's fuck it out of me."

She laughed, but I held onto her thighs, a bruising grip that I knew might mark her, but she arched into me, wanting more.

"Mark me with your nails, tell the world I'm yours."

"Hugh," she moaned, her gaze searching, then she crushed her mouth to mine. I let her feet fall so I could tug down her pants, her panties just a thin strip of cloth over her pussy.

"You're so fucking beautiful," I whispered before I lifted one leg up around my hip, and I cupped her over her panties.

"I'm really glad I do yoga for times like this," she muttered against my mouth. I smiled before kissing her again while I inserted one finger deep inside her. She was hot and wet and swollen, her panties damp.

"Are you wet for me? From my touching you? From my kiss? My Daisy's all wet and hot for me and I haven't even fucked you yet. Do you like it? Do you like it when I touch you?"

"You know I do. Please, just get me off."

"I could, or maybe I will take you right to the edge, and then pull back, teasing, just like you did at dinner tonight."

She frowned in confusion. "What?"

"All night you kept playing with your hair, biting your lip. Every time you bent over, I could see your cleavage, those beautiful tits nearly falling out of your top. I was on edge all night, and I'm sure I have a zipper mark on my dick, I was so hard. It was all I could do not to go to the bathroom and rub one out just thinking about you. But I held out, just like you're going to hold out for me. Don't come. Don't come until I tell you."

"I don't like bossy men."

"You like me. Now ride my hand, but don't come."

And she did, never breaking eye contact as she rolled her hips over my hand, and I inserted another finger, and then a third. When I slid my thumb over her clit, she shook, her eyes darkening, so I quickly slid out of her, letting her calm down.

"Hugh, I was so close."

"I told you not to come." I reached around and pinched her ass, not too hard, but definitely not light.

"Ow."

"Want me to smack it and make it better?"

She pressed her head back to the door and laughed. I kissed down her throat. I let her leg fall so I could tug on her top. The shirt wrapped around her stomach, her breasts falling into my hands.

"No bra?"

"There's one fitted into the top. It barely worked. I bounced around a lot tonight."

"Don't remind me," I muttered, before I pressed my face to her breasts and kissed and sucked. She slid her hands through my hair as I laved at her nipples, paying attention to them until they were hard little buds between my fingers and between my lips.

"You're so fucking beautiful."

"I'm so wet right now I'm pretty sure it's trailing down my thigh."

I leaned back and grinned before I bent in front of her.

"Look at you, all wet between those thighs. Looks like I need to pay more attention."

"If you don't make me come, I'm going to kick your ass."

"I think I can take care of that. We'll see. But not till I tell you."

"Why is that so hot? What is wrong with me?"

"It's because you want me."

I licked up her thighs, tasting her sweetness, and she shivered under my touch. Soon she was riding my face, her pussy wet and hot against my tongue. I spread her thighs apart, and she held onto the doorknob, trying not to fall. She wore only heels, her panties shoved to the side, and her shirt bunched at the waist.

She was a wreck and I fucking loved it.

"Come, come," I whispered against her cunt, and then she was shaking, her whole body shuddering as I slid my thumb over her clit, watching her go.

I stood, taking her in my arms, but we started laughing and I tripped over her pants, tumbling to the floor. I took the brunt of the impact, but we were both trained in how to fall, and how to not get hurt. Then she was sliding her hands into my pants, I groaned, and we were both stripping off the rest of our clothes, leaving each other naked, and wanting.

"I've never been with a guy not circumcised before," she whispered, and I grinned. "I didn't get a chance to mention it the first time. You know, with the tearing of clothes and all."

"I'm so hard right now, it doesn't really matter," I teased. She slid her hand up and down my dick, the tip extra sensitive, until her mouth covered me, and I knew I was going to blow if I wasn't careful. When I knew it was too much, I backed away, and pulled her up to me.

"Condom," I muttered, and she reached for her purse, practically climbing over me. And because they were right there, I took one nipple into my mouth. She moaned, her body nearly going limp over me, before she wiggled back down and handed me the condom.

"I've got you," I whispered.

She nodded, and I had a feeling something had just shifted. But I didn't want to think on it. So I sheathed myself in the condom and let her slide over me. She was hot and warm and tight and it took everything in me to not come right away. I let her ride me, her breasts bouncing until I had her on her back, one knee up to her shoulder, and was pounding into her. Because she was mine. Jobs didn't matter, nothing outside of this did. Her ex nor mine. It was just me and her, and I needed to claim her. It was raw and hard and everything I told myself it couldn't be.

When she came, I was right behind her, falling into one another.

I held her close, still locked together, and I knew this had changed everything.

This wasn't just for fun anymore.

As she shivered in my hold, sweaty and mine, I knew it was a fucking problem.

Chapter Twelve

Daisy

I shouldn't have been surprised as I looked down at the note in my hand.

You will be sorry, Daisy.

You will regret it.

Always.

I nearly crumpled the note, but stopped and shook my head. I hadn't even thought when I pulled the note down, thinking it was just a sticky note from one of my cousins on the door, since I was the first person into the security building that morning. But I needed it for evidence. We could do our own forensics on this, fingerprints and other things, but if it was something more than a joke, a way to annoy me, the authorities would need it. We played nice with the authorities.

"What's that?" Kane asked as he walked up. He looked over my shoulder and nearly ripped the note out of my hand before I turned away and held it away from him.

"No, I'm already an idiot and got fingerprints on it. We don't need yours, too."

My cousin scowled at me. "What the fuck are you talking about?"

I looked around, smiling at the passersby as they left the café with their coffees and breakfasts.

"Not here. Will you open the door? But try not to touch more than you have to."

He scowled at me, but put on latex gloves from his bag, and opened the door carefully.

"Let me get an evidence bag. Are you fucking kidding me right now?"

"I don't want to talk about it."

"Why is he wearing gloves? And why are you standing like you are trying to not touch anything?" Hugh asked, cementing my shitty morning.

"I'll talk about it in a minute, just don't touch the door, and fuck, I'm not thinking. Don't go inside, we should do a perimeter search."

"I already texted the crew and we're on it. Don't you dare come inside, Daisy," Kane called from the back.

Hugh looked so menacing, almost downright scary. But I knew he wouldn't hurt me. No, whatever jealousy or annoyance he felt the night before seemed gone. Now, he stood as the growly guy who wanted to know what was wrong, but I didn't have answers for him. How was I supposed to have answers for him when I barely knew what was going on myself?

"Give me a minute," I said quietly.

"Tell me. Why don't you look surprised by this? We were together all night and this morning until I dropped you off at your house to get ready. But you didn't mention this?"

His voice was low, only I knew that it would get picked up by the cameras. The cameras that hopefully caught whoever left the fucking Post-it Note.

A threatening Post-it in jagged handwriting that I recognized from the other note that had been at my house.

Hell. I should have told someone about it. But I had forgotten. So much was going on at the time that I just put it out of my mind.

And now this guy was at our work, and he could have done something to hurt my family.

I needed to get my head out of my ass and focus on this.

But, hell, I hadn't been thinking.

"Daisy," he growled again, and I narrowed my gaze at him. I might've made a mistake by not mentioning this earlier, by doing no more than making record of it and making a file and then promptly forgetting. But now I had to handle Hugh and the rest of my cousins, who were now all storming the area, checking the perimeter and doing everything that they were told via a group text for work that I clearly wasn't part of.

"I put Gus on the bakery, Ford is at the shop, and Kate is working from a table in the bakery for now, until we know if we need to evacuate or not," Noah said as he came over.

"Stop it. All of you. Here's the note," I said, holding up the evidence bag Kane had returned with.

Hugh read it quickly and scowled.

"What the fuck is this, Daisy?"

Noah gave him a look, then raised a brow at me. "What he said. What's going on?"

I shook my head as I walked into the building.

"I don't know what it is. It's a note that's threatening me."

"You didn't seem surprised by it," Hugh murmured. "What does that mean? Is this not the first one?"

Kane cursed.

"Yes, why do you look like this has happened before?" Noah asked.

"Because there was another note. It's in the file, I added it as a new case. But then we had the shooting, and the stalking case, and a thousand other things, and it has been a couple of weeks. I thought maybe it was just a neighbor who was pissed off at me for not mowing my lawn. Or leaving that crabgrass for a week because I was out of town. I didn't realize it was an actual thing."

"Are you fucking kidding me? This is what you do for a living, and you didn't think a threat towards you was an issue?"

Kane growled and stomped over to my desk and started rummaging through my files.

"Get the fuck away. I can handle this."

"Clearly you can't," Noah snarled, and went to help him look.

My cousins were acting as if I had a single little brain cell and nothing else. I hated them all.

They weren't letting me do anything.

"I didn't know it was an actual threat. I filed it, Noah was going to see it eventually when he caught up on paperwork. I forgot. I'm sorry. I've had a lot of things on my mind. But whoever left it wasn't on my security tapes."

"And the fact that he's not on your radar at all doesn't worry you? The fact that this person could seemingly get around your cameras?" Hugh said, his voice quiet. He didn't sound angry, not even concerned. There was just a deadness to it. And that probably should've worried me more than anything.

"It's honestly not that hard with the large trees I have," I snapped out. "Yes, I'm as safe as I could possibly be in that house, nobody is going to get in, but I don't have a camera on my mailbox."

"Well, that's going to fucking change," Kane snarled.

"I already handled it."

"You already handled it," Hugh repeated.

I wanted to scream or throw something, but the guys were doing a good enough job of throwing a fit. I loved my job. I loved working with my family, but the testosterone? It was killing me.

"It wasn't a fucking Post-it before. I'm sorry I didn't call out the National Guard. I'm sorry, let me rephrase that. I'm sorry I didn't fucking call out the Montgomery National Guard to help me. I didn't think it was an issue."

"But you thought it was an issue enough to file a report. At least in paperwork." Again, with that cool British accent. I was going to kick his ass. I knew there was fear walking through me, a little stress, but I was going to ignore it. I was too angry to worry about anything else.

"I get threatened nearly every time I have to work with a big bad dude who doesn't like a woman in charge. I'm used to it."

"You shouldn't have to be," Kingston said as he came inside. "I looked through the cameras already, was probably a guy, wearing a hoodie, his face was covered. He knew the exits. He's cased us out before."

A chill ran up my spine but I ignored it. Because I had to. If I didn't stand strong right then, my cousins were going to act like dumbass men. They wouldn't mean to, they wouldn't even realize they were doing it, but they would do their best to protect the little woman. Because they couldn't help it.

"That's it, you're on desk duty," Noah snapped. Ford just pinched the bridge of his nose, but I kept my gaze on Hugh's, waiting to see his reaction.

Because that was the betrayal. I knew it was coming. That Noah or any other one of my cousins would just put me on desk duty because of a single Post-it. A tiny piece of paper with only a few words, and I was suddenly a little girl who couldn't handle herself.

And they wouldn't even realize that they were cutting deep, breaking me.

"No," I said, before I finally pulled my gaze from Hugh, who still hadn't said anything. "No," I said again coolly.

"No?" Noah asked, looking far more unhinged than I felt.

"You heard me. We work together on this. You're not going to pull me off active duty for this. I followed procedure. We had a second threat and I immediately contacted you guys. I didn't try to hide it. I don't know what's going on, so maybe you could stop trying to hide me in a fucking closet, and help me figure out who's sending me a damn Post-it. They're not on camera, and the only prints on there other than mine will be his, unless he was wearing gloves too. So, let's figure that out."

"What's happening?" a familiar voice said from the doorway.

Of course. Why wouldn't my humiliation pile on? I turned to see Crew standing there, a large box by his feet.

"I heard yelling when I was over there dropping off art for my installation. Everything okay?"

"It's none of your concern," I snapped.

Crew didn't even blink at my tone, he just looked at Hugh and raised a brow.

"What's going on with her?"

"Someone threatened her in a note. Maybe a stalker, we don't know. But her cousins are now acting like Neanderthals and not listening to her, and Daisy is screaming at air because no one will listen."

Crew nodded before he scowled in my direction. "This wasn't the first time?" he asked, his voice so calm and rational that I wanted to rip his face off.

"Out. You have no say in this."

"I'm your friend. I think I have a say in this."

"You really don't. None of you do. I did what I was supposed to do, and if you pull me off this, I'm walking. I will leave this company. I'm not going to deal with this. I had to deal with you all walking on eggshells after I got hurt, I'm not going to deal with you thinking that I am so weak that I can't handle a simple fucking note."

"You weren't handling it at all," Noah snarled.

"Okay, okay, let's stop, think. Readjust," Kane said.

"Kane's right. And Daisy, we didn't treat you any differently after you got hurt," Kingston replied.

"That's a fucking lie and we all know it. You guys were so worried about me that you didn't even ask if I was feeling okay. You were afraid I was going to take your head off."

"You might have," Noah snapped.

"And? You and Ford get in a grumbly fight about who got the last cookie from Greer, and then you guys get growly, and we ask you shit. We ask you if you're doing okay. We all snap and growl at each other because we're in high-stakes situations so of course we get angry and we talk it out. But you guys never did. And here we are, fighting over one tiny little note."

"Two," Noah corrected.

I snarled. "Two. I did what I was supposed to. I'm doing what I'm supposed to. But if you kick me off this? If you hide me behind bubble wrap because you don't think I'm strong enough? Then I never should've worked with you guys in the first place. I'm done. Done."

I turned to leave, but Hugh was blocking my path.

"Don't touch me," I growled.

"Breathe."

"If you tell me to calm down, I'm going to snap."

"I wouldn't dare," Hugh said, his accent so pompous and upper crust, I knew he was trying to make me smile.

Damn the man for letting it work.

"I believe, as an outsider, I have something to add to this. And please, don't interrupt me. I may be new, but I know the rules. I know the way things should work. From what I can tell, Daisy did exactly what she was supposed to do, except for maybe not mentioning it." He looked down at me expectantly.

"Fine."

"I realize we've all been busy, and maybe that's on us. I wasn't here after the accident so I can't tell you how everything was right after. But I can see a very competent group working together and talking things out. Drama always hits companies and families, put them together and I'd say they'd explode, but that's probably a bad metaphor."

I looked at him incredulously, wondering how he could even joke about that, but I realized he was trying to actually calm us down.

Damn the man.

"Now, I'm going to go take Daisy here and get her a bloody cup of coffee. Look what you made me do, now I'm a stereotype. Fuck it. Talk it out, figure out what you're going to do. Because there might be a credible threat. And we are going to work on it. But if you put her behind a desk, I won't say you have to deal with me, because I'm not that type of guy. But I'm also not going to get in her way when she kicks your ass."

Without waiting for a reply, he tugged on my shoulder, and both he and Crew led me out of the office.

"You handled them nicely," Crew said.

Hugh glared at him.

"Well, I wasn't about to let you do it."

"No. No testosterone wars right now. I cannot handle it. You can whip your dicks out and compare them later." I paused. "I might want to watch that." And then I burst out laughing, because if I didn't, I would cry.

"Shit, Daisy. I'd hug you right now, but the big British dude might kick my ass."

"You are very correct."

"Seriously though, you need me, I'm there for you. But I'm going to get out of your way because I know you better. But you'll call me later?"

I didn't meet his gaze, I just nodded, my hands fisted at my side.

"Daisy?"

"I don't want coffee. I don't want to look at anyone. I need a minute."

Hugh nodded and Crew walked back to the art gallery. I took a deep breath and let it out slowly.

"I'd say thanks for sticking up for me, but I don't know what else to say right now."

"You don't have to say thank you. I'm pissed off at your cousins too."

"Why? They're probably doing what you wanted."

"What I wanted was to know what was happening, but you seemed to be handling it just fine."

I looked up at him. "I don't know if that's sarcasm or not. I'm too annoyed to figure it out."

"It's not. We're going to figure it out. Do you know who's sending the notes?"

I shook my head. "I've pissed off a lot of people. I don't mean to. But a woman in my position? There're a lot of guys who get the wrong impression."

His jaw tightened and he nodded. "That's what I thought. I'll help you go through them. One by one, when we're not out in the field. Because we both know you're not going on desk duty."

"I was truthful though. I'd walk. It would break every bit of me to do it, but I would walk."

"I know. Let's make sure that doesn't happen."

"It won't," Noah said from behind me, but I didn't

turn. "I'm an idiot. I'm sorry. Do you want me to grovel? I got good at groveling with Greer and Ford."

"He's actually quite an expert," Ford added, and I let out a small laugh, relieved that we were getting back to normal. Whatever our normal was.

"Don't ever do that again," I said as I turned to him. "Don't threaten to put me behind a desk because you're scared. I won't take it."

"You're right. I was an idiot. I *am* an idiot. Let's figure this out, okay?" Then he looked between me and Hugh and raised a brow. "And then you're going to tell me whatever the fuck this is, because this is a lot right now, and I haven't had my coffee yet."

I wanted to cry, but I didn't. Mostly because it would ruin the moment. I looked at all my cousins, and then at Hugh and the rest of the team as we went back to our office.

Because something was wrong. I didn't know what it was, I didn't know where it was coming from, but we would figure it out. Together.

Walking away from this would break me. I had been truthful when I said that to Hugh.

And I didn't want to walk away. Not from this place, not from my family.

And not from Hugh.

That was the scariest part of all.

Chapter Thirteen

Hugh

Apparently, taking your aggression out on a wooden slab with a target painted on it was something Americans did. Or at least these Americans. I'd lived here for a few years now, so you would've thought I'd know all of the intricacies of what it meant to be an American man with a temper. But apparently I hadn't.

For instance, I hadn't realized how fun it was to toss an ax towards a target while you were thinking about somebody you hated. For instance, Post-it Note man. I didn't know his name, didn't know his face, but every time I imagined that little hoodie-wearing Post-it loving man at the end of that target? I hit near or on the bullseye.

I was kicking ass, if I did say so myself.

"Where did you learn how to throw an ax? I'm a little worried."

"You should be worried," I said to Kane as I tossed another ax and hit dead on.

The siren went off and we all laughed before I sat back down at the picnic table, and watched Kingston go up for his round.

"I really wish Daisy could've been here for this," Crew said as he sat beside me, sipping his beer.

I nodded, as the others spoke up in protest.

"We had already scheduled this," Ford said.

"I invited her. She told me to fuck off," Noah laughed.

"That's our Daisy," Gus said, leaning back against the wall.

"I know we said it was guy's night, but she could have come." Ford grimaced. "Does that sound like I'm saying she's one of the guys? Hell. Why do I feel like we fucked up more than just today?"

I cleared my throat, playing with the label on Crew's empty beer bottle. "She's with the girls tonight. They're doing a pre-bachelorette party for Raven or something."

Everyone stared at me and I sighed. "We all know by

now that Daisy and I are seeing each other. Let us not make it a thing, shall we?"

They looked at each other and then back at me. "I didn't say a thing." Ford cleared his throat.

There was a thing that happened when a group of men who were all related, especially with Montgomery genes, just stared at you. They knew things. They didn't have to say a damn thing, and suddenly you were under the spotlight and there was no getting out of it.

"Would you like us to ask what your intentions are with our cousin?" Kane asked, sipping his beer so casually it had to be fake.

"No, I really don't want that."

"I don't know, I feel like we should say *something*," Kingston added, meeting Kane's gaze before they both turned to me as one.

I held back a shudder. "You know, sometimes I swear the two of you are twins."

Noah laughed. "People say that often, though technically they're second cousins."

"We just like to scare people. We always dress alike on Halloween, mostly to annoy our family."

"Oh, we are annoyed," Noah said with a sigh.

"Seriously though. From what I can see, you and Daisy seemed to have known each other before I hired you. You want to talk about that?"

I just sipped my beer as Crew chuckled beside me.

Damn man.

“No, I’d say ask Daisy, but I don’t want to have to kick your ass. Although she could do it herself.”

“Damn right,” Crew mumbled into his beer.

“Now you say something?”

“Hey, I’m best friends with a Montgomery who happens not to be here, you just can’t get away from them.”

I nearly choked on my beer. “Wait, there’s another of them?”

They all laughed as I stared incredulously.

“Which one are you friends with?”

“Lex. Don’t worry, he’s not here. He has better things to do than to deal with all of you.”

“Oh. Then why are you here?” I asked.

Crew just grinned. “Because I wanted to see what happened when you got surrounded by the Montgomerys. You know they wanted to ask you about Daisy.”

“There’s nothing to ask about.”

“You seem to be super protective and touchy with my cousin,” Kane said.

“And I don’t really think it’s any of your business.”

“Wrong move there,” Crew mumbled.

“And on that note, I have to get home. I left my pregnant wife to see this interrogation, and it’s taking too long. Text me the results?" Gus asked as he gave us a two-finger salute and headed out.

"He's giving up so easily? Fatherhood has weakened him," Kane said with a laugh.

"Nothing about becoming a father makes you weak." I shook my head, then checked my phone. Lucy was hanging out with Nora again tonight, but I was just having one beer and a quick dinner before I picked her up. I missed hanging out with my kid, but she was making a whole group of friends. It seemed like I was doing the same thing. Odd. I hadn't planned on that, but here we were. Life was changing, we were fitting in. And I was currently being interrogated by some of Daisy's family. Apparently by only a small slice, which was a bit worrying.

"Is she at Alex and Tabby's house?" Kane asked, and I looked up.

"Are they your aunt and uncle?" I asked, trying to fit the family tree together again.

"Close enough," Kane replied, and everybody laughed. "Technically, Daisy and I are first cousins, if that helps."

I pinched the bridge of my nose. "And Lex?"

"A whole other set of Montgomerys," Crew put in. "Really, don't think about it. Just know they think of themselves as cousins in a generation, and go with it."

"Do you have a family tree on a wall somewhere?"

"Actually, my grandparents do," Noah said. "It's a tapestry that Aunt Tabby made." Noah cleared his throat. "Tabby is Sebastian's mom. You know, the house your daughter is currently playing at?"

I nodded. "That makes sense. Tabby seems like the craftiest Montgomery." I frowned. "That sounded a lot more malicious than I meant," I said with a laugh.

"No, no, you're right," Noah said. "It's true. We're all a bit crafty in our own way."

"Some more than others," Crew mumbled into his beer.

"It's just so odd to me that you guys are all so close. That you all seem to get along."

Everybody looked at each other, then at me. "You saw the fight we just had? Yes, Daisy might've forgiven us, but it's still going to be around for a while. We're going to have to grovel." Kingston shook his head. "We get along. We love each other. But sometimes we don't like each other. And that's okay."

"Some of us have moved away and come back; not all of us live here right now. We just happen to like it here. And we like working together. There's always going to be conflict in jobs. When you add family to it, it gets a little more complicated."

"It's just what we do," Noah added.

"And when you add in people like me who have big families of my own? It gets even worse."

There was something in his tone that worried me, and I leaned forward. "Are you okay, Ford?"

Ford tipped the rest of his beer back and shook his head.

"Not so much. If you think Montgomery family drama is big? That's nothing. They're sweet and happy even as they're burning down the world to save each other. Mine just likes to tear at each other. That's the Cage family for you. Full of secrets and drama, and it makes me want to pull my fucking hair out."

"Don't do that, babe. You wouldn't like it. I guess you would look sexy bald, but I like your hair." As if proving his point, Noah pushed Ford's hair back from his face and smiled.

"I guess a bald Ford wouldn't be too bad," I added, and Ford's lips twitched.

"That ginger hair of yours seems to be working on Daisy."

"It's the accent," Kingston added.

"I can't help it that I'm a catch," I said with a laugh.

"Single dad? Check. Ginger? Check. British accent? Check." Kane counted on his fingers. "It's actually a little annoying. Thankfully you found a family member to hook up with or whatever, so we aren't competing for the same women."

"There wouldn't be a fight," I said so casually that Crew nearly snorted beer out of his nose.

"Oh, I like you. I'm glad I don't have to punch your face in."

I looked at him and then the others, who all looked oddly serious.

"You're not serious, are you?" I asked.

"You hurt Daisy, we kick your ass," Noah said with a shrug. "I mean, she could probably kick your ass harder, but maybe she'd let us have a piece."

"I'm not going to hurt her."

"Should we ask what your intentions are then?" Ford asked.

I frowned. "Is it any of your business?" I asked, my voice low.

"See, that's going to be a problem. Of course, it's our fucking business. She's family."

I sighed and rubbed my temple. "Like I said before, whatever is going on between me and Daisy is just between us."

"That's a lie," Crew said.

I looked at him, surprised. "Really, you're going to be the one to say something?"

"When Daisy and I were dating? They were all up in our business. When we broke up? I had to deal with the testosterone thing, but because Daisy and I are still friends and remained friends throughout the breakup, it wasn't a big deal. But you have a whole lot to lose. I haven't met your kid, but you seem to be a good dad. I don't know why you're here, why things are working out the way they are. But I know Daisy's childhood. She's told me enough of it. And they all know it. You wouldn't risk your daughter for something that's casual."

My stomach tightened and I swallowed. "You're right, I wouldn't."

"And Lucy has met her? I mean, I assume so because Lucy said something at the park and it passed along the phone tree," Kingston said.

I sighed and rubbed my temple. "I'm not good at the single dad thing." I paused. "I didn't have full custody until recently. My ex did. We were married for just long enough for me to get citizenship, but that's not why we got married."

"Shit," Kane said with a wince. "Lucy?"

"Yep. We thought we'd try it out, it didn't work out. My ex got full custody. Until she decided to get married again and start over and didn't want her daughter anymore."

The look of raw anger over every single face here calmed me. Because they got it. None of these men would ever do that to their kid or anyone they loved.

"I know why you moved out here. At least about closing up your business. Didn't realize the whole story."

I looked at Noah and raised a brow. "Like you don't do a background check."

"Background checks don't have feelings. Emotions. I

knew about Lucy, of course. Though I didn't know the circumstances. But as you've already seen, we Montgomerys reel you in. It seems like Nora's doing a good job with Lucy."

I laughed. "I swear those two are thick as thieves, and Nora's friends are bringing her in too. I was so worried my daughter wasn't going to be able to make friends or figure out how to live in this new state and this new world, and yet here she is, with best friends forever, as she puts it."

"And you're hanging out with us. And seeing Daisy. You're fitting in too," Kane added.

I snorted. "I don't think it was supposed to be like this."

"It never is," Crew said at my side.

"So, you going to tell us how you met?" Kingston asked.

I shook my head. "Oh fuck no. Not even a little. Sorry."

We laughed a bit, and my phone rang.

I pulled it out and chugged the last of my water.

"It's my kid. I should go."

They all said their goodbyes, and I felt a little closer to the group, not as awkward as it had been. I had guy friends before, of course. But this felt different. In that more adult way where friendships came and went, but some of them stuck.

"Hey," I said as Alex Montgomery's face slid over the screen.

"Hey, there's someone who wants to speak to you." The bearded man slid off to the side, and Lucy's face filled the screen.

"Hi, Daddy!"

"Hey, baby girl."

"Is it okay if I stay the night? I know I should've asked before, but then Nora and I are here playing with a fort with her grandma and grandpa and it's so much fun. Can I?"

"I don't want to take up so much of their time. You've spent the night with Nora three times now and we haven't reciprocated."

"Next time then at our house." She smiled so widely I was afraid I'd gotten caught in a trap. Perhaps I had. She was learning the ways of the Montgomerys and I needed to catch up.

"It's really okay," Tabby Montgomery said as she came on the screen. "We'd love to have her. We always have extra things for all of the kids. I probably should've called you privately before she got on the phone, but I misjudged the timing." She laughed as she said it, and then I saw her lean back into her husband's arms. The two seemed just as in love as they must've been when they first met. It was nice, seeing so many functional families around Lucy.

"That'd be great, and I'll talk to Sebastian and Raven about Nora. Well damn, I guess I should probably talk to them before the wedding, since I don't know the plans for that."

"We'll keep in touch and make it work. Nora's staying with us during their honeymoon, and we'd love the help." She winked as she said it.

I just smiled. "Well, thank you."

"Thank you, Daddy. I love you and goodnight."

"I love you too, bug. Be safe, okay?"

"Always. Love you to the moon."

"To the stars," I whispered as she hung up. I rubbed my hand over my heart.

I loved that kid. She stressed me out, made me worried, and I knew would do the same until the end of my days, but I loved her so damn much.

I slid my phone into my pocket and realized I had a whole night off and I didn't have to work tomorrow until later in the evening. We had a night off, and that meant I had the morning off; instead of Saturday cartoons and Lucy's fun mornings, I could do whatever I wanted.

So that's how I found myself in the car driving towards Daisy's house without even thinking. She was probably still out with her friends. I should probably text her and check in.

I wanted more. I needed more.

A part of me needed to keep her safe too. Because

someone was threatening her. Even if it was just a fucking Post-it Note. I needed to figure out who it was before they hurt her. I'd be damned if that ever happened.

I pulled into her driveway, happy to see that her living room light was on. Of course, that could've just been a security measure, but I hoped she was home. And because I knew she had cameras up, she would know I was here before I even got out of the car. Good.

Because I wanted her, but I didn't want to worry her.

When I got out of the car, I wasn't surprised she opened the door before I even reached it.

"And what are you doing here?" she asked, a glass of wine in hand and a brow raised.

"Lucy's with Nora's grandparents for the night. I seem to find myself alone."

She smiled and tilted her head back as I hovered over her.

"That sounds like a predicament."

"I have a whole night free. Whatever shall I do?"

And then my mouth was on hers, and the door was closing behind us, and I let myself breathe.

Just for the night, I let myself be.

Chapter Fourteen

DAISY

"This is a big thing, isn't it?"

I looked over at Brooke. I knew exactly what she was talking about, but there was no way I was discussing it.

"I have no idea what you're speaking of."

My friend raised a brow at me and shook her head. "Really? That's what you're going with." She smoothed her hands over her hips, both of us taking up space in the mirror to check our dresses.

We were here for a wedding. Odd to think this was

my second wedding in so many months, but it was a wedding that I was excited for.

My cousin Sebastian had seen the worst, dealt with the worst. And yet here he was, about to take that next step with one of my best friends.

I still couldn't believe it had been over five years since he'd lost Marley.

I still remembered Marley's laugh, the way she would shy away and be overwhelmed by the sheer amount of Sebastian's family. But she had always been there, quiet, but engaged. Part of us.

And when we lost her, it was like losing a limb. Part of our souls. Sebastian had gone and figured out how strong he was, not for himself, but because of Nora. His little girl needed him, and he stepped up to the plate. Just like our family had done for him. We hadn't let him do this alone, hadn't let him grieve or raise Nora by himself. But now he had found his new happy ever after. His Raven. The fact that Raven had also been friends with Sebastian and Marley when they were younger made everything feel full circle. It was a gift, the love between the two of them. It was his second chance, as well as Nora's. Because she loved Raven with all of her little heart.

Nora was such a wonderful child and made friends wherever she went.

Which was why Brooke was standing there, looking at me and not her own reflection.

Because Nora had brought one of her friends, and that friend happened to have a single father, who was sort of my date.

"Are you lost in thought about the wedding that is about to happen? Or about a certain single dad who I know is going to be out there tonight?"

I narrowed my gaze at Brooke. "Were you always this tenacious or have we rubbed off on you as a family?"

We were here for this wedding for two of my favorite people, and I was standing by another of my favorite people. I was so damn blessed. Brooke had a second chance with my cousin, because sometimes fate was great like that.

Lake and Nick were happy and in love and healed. Soon they would be having a baby, and Noah and his two loves were engaged, and we'd be going through this whole circus again. It was never too much. It never felt as if things were over the top, but people were moving on and starting families, and somehow I was here with a date. With his daughter. It didn't really make sense how I had gotten here.

Was I dating Hugh? Was he my boyfriend?

"I really want to know what's going on inside your mind right now because it looks like your brain is spinning a thousand miles an hour."

I looked over at Brooke, and asked, "Is he my boyfriend?"

Brooke looked at me, blinked, and burst out laughing.

"I don't know if I appreciate that reaction. I mean, I could use a little support here."

"Oh, I've got your support. Yes, he's your boyfriend. You guys are what, seeing each other a couple of times a week? Eating together, spending time together. And not just for work things?"

"Maybe."

"And now he's here at a wedding with you?"

"Technically Nora invited Lucy because Nora is standing up between Raven and Sebastian for the wedding. Which, can I just say, is the cutest thing ever. I know Nora wanted to be a flower girl, but her standing with them for the wedding? It's a family." I wiped tears from the corner of my eyes, annoyed with myself. "If I ruin this makeup already, I'm going to be very upset with myself."

Brooke smiled. "It is adorable and it's perfect for them. Because they're not forgetting where they came from, but they are looking to the future. We didn't have Luke stand with us like that, but he ended up in Leif's arms for the end of it." Brooke wiped away tears as I remembered their wedding. Luke was Brooke's son from a previous relationship, but called Leif Daddy now, and had been a big part of their wedding. Just like Nora was now. Second chances didn't come often, but it seemed that my family was finding theirs.

"Okay, Hugh is here as my date. And I sort of invited him, but mostly because Nora had already invited Lucy, so I wanted him to come with his daughter. Things are just so complicated. How did he become my boyfriend? Are we allowed to say boyfriend at our age?"

"I don't know why you're acting as if we're eighty. And by the way, eighty-year-olds have boyfriends. Live in the moment. Claim the title. You are dating. Have you guys introduced yourselves to anyone else?"

I shook my head. "Not really. We sort of just know everybody we hang out with. Hugh's new to the area. It's not like he really knows anyone to introduce me to. His friends are my friends. Which is going to get really complicated when this whole thing explodes."

"If. Not when. Let's not put that out there into the universe."

I nodded, wringing my hands in front of me. "I'm really not good at this. I think the most serious relationship I've ever had was with Crew, and I don't know if that counts."

"Because you guys are still friends who hang out and work out? How is Hugh handling that?"

"Oddly okay. Mostly because they get to gripe about me." I didn't bring up the notes, or the fact that over the past weeks we hadn't learned anything. Maybe it was a person who wanted to scare me, but there hadn't been anything else. We'd only had issues from that rival security company, but even then, I wasn't the center of it. Everybody had somewhat stopped growling around me, trying to protect me from an unknown force. We were still working and everything felt normal.

Including the fact that I was seeing Hugh.

"It's okay, you know. To be happy. I didn't let myself think that for a long time. But I'm glad you are. At least I hope you are."

I bit my lip and nodded. "I'm going to try. I'm going to try not to think of the worst as well. Not that that's easy."

"Tell me about it."

"Knock, knock." I turned to see Kane standing there, a smile on his face, but there was something in his eyes. He had been hiding something. And while I wanted to force him to tell me, I knew he wouldn't. He was growlier than I was. And that was saying something. If he wanted to have a secret, I would let him. But I hoped when it was time, if he was hurting, he would come to us. I just wanted him to be okay.

"We should be getting out there. You ready?" he asked us both and I nodded, taking Brooke's hands.

"Let's go, it's time for a wedding."

"I hope I don't sob the entire time. I don't know why weddings get to me."

"I don't know either. They're just saying a few words to each other before we get to eat cake. The world already knows they love each other. That they have each other. Why do they need to have a whole party for it?" Kane asked, and I met Brooke's gaze, wondering where his hostility was coming from, but we didn't ask, because standing in front of us were two people that took my breath away.

"Babe," Leif said as he held out his hand, and Brooke hugged her husband before they headed into the ceremony, taking their seats. Kane mumbled something at my side, but I didn't hear it. I just saw him walking away, and then I was alone with Hugh.

Again.

"You look astonishing," he whispered.

There was something about that accent that sent shivers down my spine.

I wore a champagne-colored dress, something that complemented the colors of the wedding, but as I wasn't an attendant, I didn't have to match exactly. Only Greer and Noah were standing up for them. We outnumbered Raven's family by a lot, so we didn't bother with bride or groom's side seating. Plus, Raven was one of ours anyway.

Hugh stood there in his gray suit that hugged his

body and made me want to rip it off him. I loved a man in a good suit. And I had seen Hugh in them before, since we did some bodyguard services where we needed to be dressed up, but I had never seen him like this.

I loved the way he looked in jeans, in gray sweats, in anything, in nothing. But the suit?

"We should go sit down before I press you up against the wall and do something I shouldn't," he grumbled.

"Honestly, I was thinking the same thing."

He reached out and trailed his finger along my jawline, and I shivered at his touch.

There was just something about him. Just *something*. And I knew I needed to rein it in if I wanted to stay in control.

"We should go sit down."

"We should." I cleared my throat. "Where's Lucy?"

Hugh grinned, his smile so bright at the mention of his daughter, that the ice around my heart began to crack, just a little.

Damn it. I couldn't fall for him. I couldn't love him. Not when I didn't know what was coming. But it was just so hard not to.

But that was a problem for future Daisy.

"She is sitting with Nora's grandparents, even though she was supposed to be my date for the wedding. However, she wanted to support them since Nora wouldn't be sitting with them." He rolled his eyes. "As if they don't have other grandchildren."

"That is seriously the sweetest thing ever."

"True, but now I don't have a date."

I raised a brow. "I'm pretty sure I can fill in. If Lucy's okay with that."

"Oh, she's okay with it. In fact, I'm pretty sure she demanded it."

He smiled and took my hand, and we made our way inside.

We sat by Kane and Kingston.

"Are you really trolling for women at a wedding?"

Kingston scoffed. "It's a little difficult when most of the attendees are family members or already taken. But don't worry, I see a couple of Raven's friends from school. This could be interesting." He looked at Kane. "What do you say?"

Kane shook his head. "All yours. I'm just here for the cake."

I frowned, wondering what was going on with him, but I ignored it for now, paying attention to Hugh. He slid his hand over my knee and tension slid through me before I turned my attention back on the ceremony.

When the music began, I swallowed back tears. I needed to be strong, even though from the way people were sniffling around us, I wasn't the only one having a hard time.

Because everyone in this room knew the enormity of what was happening, and when Hugh handed me a linen cloth to wipe my tears, I leaned on him and watched two people that I adored profess their love and promises to each other, with little Nora bouncing between them, agreeing to watch over them no matter what.

They loved each other, the two of them, and I was forever grateful that I was part of this.

That I could watch this.

And I could feel Hugh's heat against me.

And I let myself fall just that much more. Even if I knew I shouldn't.

As the bride and groom danced across the dance floor, I smiled into my champagne and looked up at Hugh.

"What?" I asked, knowing that people's attention was on the couple in front of us. I'd never brought a date to a wedding before, so I hadn't known what to expect. But so far everybody had been giving him space and hadn't made things too complicated. However, I knew that could change at any minute. My dad was giving me a side eye every once in a while, checking out Hugh, and while they had met, they hadn't spent much time together.

"I was thinking about the fact that I met you at a wedding. It seems like we've come full circle." He had his arm around my waist and I leaned into him.

"Pretty much. And that wedding ended pretty nicely." I saw his gaze go dark. A good kind of dark. I pressed my thighs together and swallowed.

"Okay, I should stop talking or this is going to get very uncomfortable soon," Hugh mumbled as he squeezed my hip. I sipped my champagne, the cold bubbles soothing as they went down my throat.

The music changed and people went out to the dance floor, but we didn't move. We stood near the back wall.

"You know, there's a large closet on the other side of the hall. Just down that hallway."

He looked down at me and I drained the rest of my drink. He did the same, then took both glasses and set them down on a nearby table. I shivered.

Hand in hand, we tried to look casual walking through the crowd, and thankfully were ignored. Lucy was hanging out with Nora, being watched by the grandparents, and that meant we had a few moments. This was so wrong, and I didn't care.

We made it to the hallway without being stopped, and then we took off running. We were laughing like teenagers, but my heart raced and I wanted more. And then I found myself in the closet, door closed behind me, being lifted onto a shelf.

"If this buckles, we're going to have to pay for it," I said with a laugh.

Hugh grinned, and then his mouth was on mine. He slid his hands up my skirt, gripping my hips, and I spread my legs for him, letting him settle between them. He kissed me harder and harder, tongues meshing, before he was nibbling on my throat and shoulder. He pulled down the bodice of my dress, my breasts pooling into his hands. I wanted more, needed more. I gripped him over his pants and squeezed.

"Dear God," he mumbled. "If we aren't careful, I'm going to come in my pants instead of fucking you in this closet."

"At least it's a nice closet."

I slid my hand over him again, as he squeezed my thighs, kissing me gently, and then harder.

I moaned, needing more, knowing this might be all we could get. But I wanted everything.

Everything? Did I mean in this moment, or beyond?

I didn't want to think about that, and yet I couldn't help but remember how we had met.

He caught the garter. I caught the bouquet.

But it was just a superstition, it was fake. It led to this though, and I'd be damn happy if I could keep it.

But I wasn't going to say that out loud.

But then he was kissing me harder and I forgot everything else.

Until the door opened.

"Are you kidding me right now?"

We froze, and I was grateful that Hugh's back was to the door. I knew that voice, as well as the growl beside it.

"Daisy Montgomery-Knight."

"Dad?" I squeaked, and Hugh cursed.

Hugh was completely dressed, and I quickly adjusted my dress so I was decent. But he was standing between my thighs, and this couldn't get more awkward.

"I am going to go dance with your mother and we are never going to talk about this." I heard my dad walk away, as Kane cleared his throat.

"Well, I would let you two continue, but they wanted us for some more candid photos. I guess you should probably get ready. But congratulations, you're the first Montgomery at this wedding to get caught in a closet. Remember what happened at Leif's?" he asked, but before I could answer he closed the door behind him, though I could still hear his laughter.

"Oh my God. That was my dad. And my cousin. I'm going to go die now."

Hugh pressed his forehead to mine, his breaths coming in pants.

"Do you think your dad is going to kill me now? Or wait until I'm not expecting it?"

"He would never do that to Lucy," I said honestly, and Hugh looked at me before he burst out laughing. "Not the impression I wanted to have with him."

"Well, it's fine. I am steeped in mortification. I'm going to need so much therapy."

Hugh pulled me off the shelf, and then we were laughing while fixing each other's clothes.

"I'm going to need a minute," Hugh said, and I looked down at his crotch and the very hard erection pressing through his pants.

"Oh my."

"Pretty much. You do this to me. And I cannot believe I just left my kid out there dancing with her best friend while I'm making out with you in a closet."

I saw the annoyance in his gaze. Was it at me? Or the situation?

"I'm sorry. We just lost our minds for a bit."

"Yeah. Seems like we did."

He didn't say anything else. He just let out a deep breath, and then we left the closet, thankfully to an empty hallway.

He didn't hold my hand, just walked by my side as we went back to the reception, and for some reason fear settled into my belly.

I had done the unthinkable. I had fallen for Hugh.

Chapter Fifteen

Hugh

"You're at another Montgomery event. Soon you're going to end up with the tattoo we all have."

I looked at Kane and raised a brow. "Excuse me?" I asked, feeling awkward. Lucy was hanging out with Nora in the kids' area as I found myself at yet another Montgomery event. Just last week we were at a wedding, and now we were at an engagement party. The triad of Noah, Greer, and Ford had put off the engagement party for a few months so the wedding could be the main event of the season. But now that all of Greer's brothers were in town, as well as Ford's siblings, they decided to have it.

I still wasn't sure how I had gotten the invite. Because it had nothing to do with Lucy.

"Wait, you all have the same tattoo?"

Kane just raised a brow, and I thought about the tattoos on Daisy's body. Of course, now I was thinking about Daisy naked and I needed to rein that back in or this was going to get quite uncomfortable very quickly. "Oh, the iris."

Daisy's was on her outer thigh, mixed in a bouquet of roses with thorns. It was beautiful, and I had licked every inch of it. Not that I was going to let anybody know that.

"It's not mandatory when you join the family or are born into it, but all of us who want ink have it. It started with Uncle Austin, and it sort of just spread out. It's nice. It's our little logo."

"So will Greer and Ford get one? Even though they have big families of their own?"

"Not sure. Ford probably will. He's been one of us forever, even if his brothers won't let us actually keep him."

That made my lips twitch. "How many brothers does he have?" I asked.

"He has six brothers, but did you hear about the other set?"

My eyes widen. "What do you mean other set?"

"Oh yes. Apparently the Cage family has secrets.

Including a whole separate family that nobody knew about."

I nearly dropped my drink. "Are you fucking kidding me?"

"Nope. And I know we gossip between family, but I don't know if it's really well known yet. And considering the Cage family business interests, it's going to make waves soon."

I wondered how the hell someone could do that. "So, wait, the dad had a whole secret family, and no one knew?"

"So I hear. I don't know how Ford's dealing with it. I don't even know how many there are. But, they're not here tonight. Just the main siblings. It's going to be awkward at family dinners."

"What a betrayal. I mean, my ex left her own daughter to start her own second family, but at least she had the courtesy not to hide it." I winced. "That's setting the bar really low."

"Tell me about it." Kane downed the rest of his drink and shook his head. "And the thing about it is, I'm not even surprised. People are assholes. They hide things, and they pretend that they have your best interests at heart. And then everything blows up and you don't know what you're supposed to do about it."

"What are you talking about?" I asked. "What's wrong, Kane? That sounded pointed at something else."

He looked at me and snorted. "Just be grateful Daisy doesn't keep secrets from you. I mean, there was that whole note thing that we still haven't figured out who is behind it, but you're here at a family event again. I don't know how serious the two of you are, but I like that you're here. For her. And you won't even have to get the tattoo if it gets serious."

"Well..." I wasn't sure what I was supposed to say to that, and just let my voice trail off.

"You're not going to hurt Daisy, are you?" he asked, his voice low.

"No," I said, then frowned. "We're just, we work together. We're friends. And I have Lucy to think about."

Kane gave me a disappointed look and reached for a water. "You better come up with a different answer if her dad asks. Or anyone else. Hell, come up with a different answer when you talk to Daisy."

"We are taking it slow. We're friends."

"Friends don't do what I walked in on last week," he said, referencing that lovely closet.

I still hadn't faced Daisy's father, and I didn't have any plans to. Call me chickenshit.

"I just, I was married. I got divorced. Even though I married for the wrong reasons, I got Lucy out of the deal. And she's everything to me. I don't want to hurt her."

"Daisy, or Lucy?"

I shook my head. "Both. I realized that we just had a wedding, an engagement party, but hell, Daisy and I have only been seeing each other for a few weeks. Can't we just let that be? Because Lucy's first."

"It's good that you say that. Just don't hurt Daisy, okay? She deserves to be happy."

Kane walked off, leaving me confused once again.

"Daddy!" Lucy ran up to me, arms outstretched, so I set my drink down and caught her as she jumped.

"You're getting better at your aim when you leap at me," I said with a laugh as I spun her around before setting her down. I could still pick her up and toss her around; she wasn't too big for that yet, but she wasn't a baby anymore. She was a grownup, with pierced ears, bright eyes, and wearing a pretty dress. We kept getting invited to Montgomery family events, and it seemed like Lucy fit right in.

What would happen if Daisy and I broke up? Or if things got too serious?

I'd gone into this thinking I could handle it all, that I could juggle it. But what would we do if we didn't get invites to these things? I still fucking worked with them. And Lucy was now best friends with Nora and her crew.

Our lives were already so deeply entangled, that I was afraid of what it was going to do to my daughter if the worst happened.

Hell. I had thought about it, tried to be careful, but it seemed I wasn't careful enough.

"Where's Daisy?" Lucy asked, reminding me that Lucy was falling for Daisy too.

I really wasn't doing a good job with this. I needed to protect my kid.

And I needed to figure out exactly how I felt.

"Oh, she's over there talking with her cousin, Lake."

"Isn't Lake beautiful? And she let me touch her belly and I felt the baby kick. Did you know babies kick? But she won't tell me how it got in there. She said that's something you have to talk to me about." She rolled her eyes. "I don't know, maybe mommies are supposed to talk to kids about where the baby came from, but since I don't have a mommy, maybe I'll just ask Daisy. Daisy would tell me because she's like my best friend now and I love her. I don't need a mommy. But I like Daisy." She blinked innocently at me and nearly got away, before I reached out and caught her arm, still in shock at her words.

I could barely comprehend exactly what she had just said. My daughter didn't talk about her mother. Fuck everything that she had done to my kid.

But the fact that Lucy was equating Daisy to her, even saying that she didn't need a mom at the same time? We were in need of a big talk, but I didn't know if now was the best time.

"Lucy. Slow down."

"I just saw Daisy, so I was going to ask her how the baby got there."

That made me laugh, and I reached out and tugged Lucy closer. Of course, Kingston must have heard that last part, because the other man was doing a poor job at holding back laughter. I pleaded with my eyes to him for help, though I didn't know what kind of help he would give me, but he just turned tail and ran.

Coward.

"Okay, let's go sit over here." I reached the couch at the edge of the room and sat down. Lucy scrambled into my lap and began chattering a mile a minute about how she loved Daisy and Brooke and Lake and everybody. She was just so happy to be there.

"Let's talk about the whole mommy thing, okay?" I whispered.

She looked at me, no hate or worry in her gaze, looking more grownup than she needed to.

"It's okay. I know Mommy doesn't love me. And she doesn't love you. Or maybe she used to love me but changed her mind. That's sort of what the therapist said, right?"

I shook my head, wondering if we needed a new therapist.

"Your mommy made choices. Choices I don't agree with. But I love you, I want you in my life, and I'm so grateful that I get to be your daddy. It's okay to be sad about everything that happened."

"I was sad. But now I have you. And Nora and her family. I know they aren't our family, but they said they keep adopting everybody that comes near them. Or maybe they said something about spiders and webs, but I don't like spiders. So they are our family. And you being Daisy's boyfriend? That's just a bonus. At least that's what Nora said, like how Raven was a bonus until she became her mommy. And I know Daisy isn't my mommy, but I really like her. So it's okay if you wanted her to be my mommy." She said it so quickly, I wondered what the hell I had done to my daughter. Because Daisy and I hadn't talked about what we were. We had just rushed into this, trying to be the best for Lucy while also tiptoeing around the fact that we still worked together, that Daisy might be in danger, and that I was starting over. We skipped all the important steps, and now I might hurt my kid because I wasn't smart enough to figure out what the fuck was going on.

Great job, Hugh.

"Okay, baby. That's a lot to unpack."

"That's what the therapist says. But Miss Molly is great. We can unpack it with her next week." She beamed.

"I love you. And I know Nora loves you, and so does Daisy." That much I knew. I saw the love for her in

Daisy's eyes. I just hadn't let myself look deeper at any feelings she might have for me. Because I was fucking afraid.

And wasn't that an amazing thing to think? My ex had done a number on us. I had let myself love her, even if we hadn't started our relationship in the most conventional way. She had broken my heart, mostly because of how she broke my kid's heart. But she had nonetheless.

"I know Daisy loves me. And even if she's not my mommy, I love her." She shrugged, then hopped off my lap. "Nora's waving, we're going to go get cake, is that okay?" I nodded, and watched her run away, only belatedly realizing that she'd already had a slice of cake. Apparently that kid needed two slices. And I needed a fucking drink.

"What's the look on your face for?" Daisy asked as she handed over an old fashioned, as if she had read my mind.

She was so good at that. We fit into each other's lives so easily.

Everything was so damn complicated. And the thing was, it always had been. I just lied to myself so it wouldn't be.

I took a sip of the drink and nodded my thanks. "Well, Lucy was looking for you so she could ask you how the baby got into Lake's belly."

Daisy took a seat next to me and set her drink down

on the small table in front of us. "What was your answer? I mean, do I need to go hide? She's really scary."

I laughed. "That's pretty much exactly what my reaction was. I have no idea what I'm supposed to say. I know there's books on this, but she's still my baby. She's not supposed to ask where they come from yet."

"Oh gosh, is Nora asking? Maybe Brooke will know. She has kids. But they're boys. Boys are weird." She paused. "No offense."

"Oh no, girls are weirder."

"I don't know about that," she said with a laugh.

I tried to relax, only it was hard when she was at my side.

"Thanks for coming tonight. I know you don't get many Saturday nights off. Neither do I. Well, I don't schedule them off for either one of us," she said with a laugh. "But I'm grateful. And really, it's an excuse for food and dancing, but it is a lot of Montgomerys. You can leave whenever you need to. I don't want this to be too much for you."

I looked at her, trying to figure out what she wanted. What she felt.

"What?" she asked, her voice soft. "Is it too much? Are we going too fast for Lucy? I mean, I know we're having fun and things are going great, I just don't want to hurt Lucy. Nor do I want to have *that* conversation," she added, trying to lighten the mood. But something had shifted. I didn't know what she felt. What she wanted. It was all I could do not to ask. But if I did, that would change everything, so I didn't. Because I didn't know what I wanted.

The problem was, maybe I did. Maybe I wanted Daisy.

But what if she thought it was too much and she left just like my ex? What if she left Lucy?

What if she left me?

I didn't think either of us would be able to survive that. And that was a problem.

"It's not too much. Lucy likes being here."

Daisy met my gaze. "And you?"

"Daisy."

"No, don't say anything. I don't want things to get too serious while we're in the middle of this. It would just make it complicated, right?"

"Things are already complicated. And you're right, I don't want to hurt my daughter."

Daisy's eyes began to fill, and I reached out to grip her hand.

"I'm not saying we will. I'm just saying maybe when we're not surrounded by your family, we should probably figure out what's going on and actually have a talk. This isn't the best place."

Daisy nodded, then looked past me at the triad

dancing and laughing with one another, as Greer's brothers stole her away for a dance of their own.

"You're right. This isn't the greatest time. I don't know why you got so serious just then."

I reached out and cupped her face. "It's okay. I'm not going anywhere, Daisy. We should just talk."

She pulled away and I went cold.

"I really hate that phrase."

"I'm not good at the talking, so come on, let's dance." I leaned down and brushed my lips against hers, but she didn't kiss me back. She sat frozen, and I could have kicked myself.

"Daisy. Let's dance."

"Okay, I can do that."

When she was in my arms, I felt like I had misstepped. I didn't know what I wanted, and I was putting that on Daisy. I needed to fix that. Only, I wanted her in my arms. I wanted more.

Yet if I took that risk, I could hurt my kid.

I could hurt myself.

But I was really afraid if I didn't take that step, I'd hurt Daisy.

I had no idea what I was supposed to say to fix it. Or if I could fix this at all.

Chapter Sixteen

DAISY

We hadn't broken up. At least that's what I kept telling myself. No, we hadn't ended our relationship, but something had changed.

Everything was a little more awkward now, and I didn't understand why. It wasn't as if we had ended things, or never saw one another. We had. I worked with him every day. And though he was out on calls with Kingston and Kane, and I was working with Gus and Ford more often than not, we still saw each other in the office. We still brushed hands when we walked to each other's cars.

It had been a busy week, with multiple alarms going off at different warehouses we were in charge of security for. It had been a week of us trying to catch up with teens or burglars or someone trying to case places. They had all turned out to be false alarms, which was annoying to no end, but we were working our asses off. Though it wasn't just us. There seemed to be a rash of fake alarms. Just that morning I had been awoken to do a four-a.m. walkthrough because one of our priority clients had their entire alarm set off. The authorities arrived and didn't see anything, the cameras hadn't caught anything, so I did a walkthrough.

I was exhausted, desperately in need of the coffee in my hands, but I still couldn't help but think about how awkward things were with Hugh.

There hadn't been time for Hugh and me to have dinner, or see each other, or do anything more than talk briefly at work. He had a school play, parent teacher conferences with Lucy, as well as countless other things. He was a father first, and we knew that. That was his priority when we had decided to see each other. And I loved that, because he was doing the same thing my father had done for me. He had put his all into protecting his child, to being there for his child. So of course, I was going to make sure that Hugh always did that for Lucy.

But we still hadn't had the talk about what we wanted from each other. What would happen.

I hadn't told him I loved him. Maybe if I had, things would've been different, but it still felt so weird.

"You're in your head. Do you want to talk about it?"

I looked up as Aria sipped her coffee and stared at me. Sebastian's twin had the Montgomery blue eyes and a beautiful smile. I missed working with her every day, but she was so much better where she was now than she had been with us. I hated not seeing her every day, but she was working too many hours in a job she loved. That meant we didn't get to catch up as much as we wanted.

"I'm fine. Just drinking coffee. Early morning, as I told you."

It wasn't quite a lie. I was exhausted, but I hadn't told anyone about my feelings for Hugh—I had barely even admitted those feelings to myself.

I wasn't sure I was ready to put it out into the universe like that.

But knowing Aria, I wasn't sure I had a choice.

"I am headed next door to the art shop to talk with another one of our cousins. But before I do that, I'm going to get the truth out of you."

"What truth? I'm just tired."

"There's something in your eyes. What's going on

with you and Hugh? You guys looked great at the wedding and the engagement party. I was surprised you brought him to both."

I winced and sipped my lifeline, the coffee cool but exactly what I needed in this moment.

"I know you don't want to talk about him, but he's not here right now and all the customers in here are paying attention to their phones and aren't related to us or the companies. Greer and Raven aren't even behind the counter, as one of them is on their honeymoon and the other has the day off. It's just us. Nobody can hear but me. Talk to me."

I pressed my lips together before I sighed. "I'm afraid he wants to break up with me because it's too complicated." I set the cup down. "Which I wouldn't blame him for. We are complicated. I'm his boss and yet not his boss at the same time. He's slowly integrating himself into our friends and family, and because he's new here, I'm not sure he even has friends outside of our group. So if he breaks up with me, he's going to lose that as well. And Lucy? She and Nora are best friends. We're never going to be able to separate them. So no matter what I do, he will always be there. If he wants to end it, if he needs to end it, it's not an actual ending. It's just me not being able to be with him anymore, but still being forced to always be with him. I knew that this could happen. We had even said it would be awkward but we were going to try anyway because we were adults and we could handle this. But I sure as hell don't feel like an adult right now. I just feel so tired and as if I'm waiting for the other shoe to drop or waiting for everything to end."

Aria looked at me and shook her head, smiling sadly. "You love him. You really love him. It's not just attraction, you're in love with him. Big L and everything."

I looked around, as if someone were listening in, but they weren't. "Yes, okay. I'm in love with him. I have no idea how it happened, because I was telling myself we were good at just being with each other and not letting things get too crazy, and suddenly I'm thinking about him far too much, and we're working well together, we hang out well together, I love hanging out with his kid. Seriously, Lucy is such a delight. And I know that I'm not her mom. She does not need me like that."

"Are you sure about that?" Aria interrupted and I shook my head.

"I can't even let myself think things like that because if I do, it hurts my stomach. I don't know anything other than I'm nervous. I don't want to lose him. I love him. And I'm so afraid that if I tell him, it's going to ruin everything. I'm also afraid that if I don't tell him, I'm just lying to myself. I've never been in this situation before. I have watched so many of our family members and friends fall in love, and seen how easy and hard it is all at once, and not once did I actually ever think that I would be in this situation."

"I thought you and Crew..." She shook her head. "I thought you were each other's."

I shook my head. "No. Crew and I liked each other, but we realized quickly that we were better as friends. I mean the sex was great. I can't lie. We had great chemistry, but you're allowed to have that without wanting something more. And he and Hugh are starting to become friends too. See? It's a tangled web."

"And you are in the center of that web. You owe it to yourself to tell him what you feel. I know that's saying a lot for someone who's never actually been in love. But you deserve happiness. You both do. Lucy does too."

"And if I tell him I love him, that means it's all happy ever after and suddenly I'm with a man forever who has a daughter and everything just works out?"

"It worked out for your parents."

I shook my head. "We were lucky. I'm really afraid that luck doesn't happen twice."

"All of these what-ifs aren't helping. You need to talk to him. I know it sucks. I know it's scary. I'm not going to ask you what you have to lose because we all know that question's ridiculous. There's always something to lose."

"But you're right. If I don't tell him, then he doesn't have all the information." I said it quickly, a little high-pitched. "And honestly, I can't imagine my life without him. I don't know how it happened. I love him. I love the way that he is with Lucy, with me. I love how smart he is. How great he is with work. I mean, it was always going to be complicated. Ever since that first dance it was going to be complicated. But I should tell him before he decides I'm too much and walks away. I need to tell him. It's not fair to him."

"It's not fair to you to keep it inside either."

I reached over the table and squeezed her hand. "I love you."

"You should be telling him that. But I love you too." Aria winked as she drank the last of her coffee.

"I know you got that to go so you could go open up the office. So get in there. Although are you supposed to be alone?" she asked, narrowing her gaze.

"Kingston is on his way in too. Don't worry, I'm not alone at the office."

"If you say so."

My phone buzzed and I looked down at the readout, my heart expanding and breaking all at once.

"Who is it?" Aria asked, standing up to look over my shoulder. She put her hand on her chest over her heart and let out a happy sigh.

"That is the sweetest thing."

Hugh: *Dinner tonight?*

And attached was a piece of artwork from Lucy, asking me to dinner.

For some reason tears pricked the back of my eyelids, and I wiped them away quickly, texting back.

Me: *Count me in.*

"See? Maybe it's not as dire as you think."

I swallowed but nodded. "You're right. Maybe I could have everything. And not lose it all."

"Come on, I need to head into work and so do you. You said Kingston's on his way?"

"He is. I'll talk to you soon."

"And give me all the details."

I grimaced, suddenly afraid and nervous, but I would do it. I would tell him.

I wanted him. I loved him. And I had to take that risk.

I walked out of the coffee shop, and then cursed when I remembered I had folders I needed in the trunk of my car. I went back to the parking lot, my mind thinking about how dinner tonight was going to go. I would talk to Hugh today at work about it, and then I would figure out how to tell him I loved him.

Because I had to.

The first hit came out of nowhere, slamming me on the back of the head. I ran into the wall, my face dragged along the brick. Instincts kicked in, and I slammed my head back, hearing the guy curse, blood pooling on my shoulder from where I had broken his nose. I whirled to kick out as another hand pulled at my hair, tugging me back.

"Bitch."

My phone had fallen when I was hit, and I reached for it, trying to dial the emergency code. We were in a well-lit parking lot but were behind the building and it was still early enough that the trees covered us. This would be caught on the security cams, and I could take them. I could.

I lashed out, hitting one of the men as he kicked me in the kidney, and I went to my knees, gasping for breath at the sharp pain.

I gagged, forcing myself to stand up, and knocked one man out, and then came at another.

But I realized there were five of them, and only one of me.

And there was no one else in this parking lot.

I attacked, taking another man out. The snap of bone underneath the pressure of my arm sent a delight through me. He was going to feel that for a long time.

I would get through this. I had to get through this.

Who the hell were these guys?

Adrenaline surged and I kept fighting, and I reached for the phone again, only to be pulled back, hands around my throat.

I kicked out, but my eyes widened and electric

shocks sang through my body as the taser slammed into me.

I shook, my teeth clenching, and then I was on the ground, hand reaching for my phone.

And then there was nothing.

Chapter Seventeen

Hugh

"And she said yes? She's really going to come to dinner?"

"Yes, she's really going to come to dinner. I promise."

"Isn't Daisy the best?" Nora asked, and I looked between the two girls, exhausted from the slumber party on a school night, and the fact that I was still nervous about seeing Daisy.

I had seen her all week at work, and we had spoken every day. But I was getting my head out of my ass and was going to tell her I wanted her in our lives.

Lucy had already explained that she wanted Daisy in

our lives. I was the one trailing behind. So, we would make this happen. For Lucy. For me. And I hoped to hell for Daisy.

"I showed her your artwork too. She's coming over for dinner, and then we'll have a movie night. Does that sound fun?"

"That sounds like the best, Daddy. I can't wait. I love Daisy." Lucy turned to Nora and beamed. "Maybe she'll be like Raven and be here all the time. I like it when she's here."

The two of them talked a mile a minute, and I rubbed my temples. I didn't know how people dealt with more than one kid—Lucy was running circles around me, and I couldn't keep up.

But it didn't matter, all that did was that I didn't screw anything up.

That I didn't ruin this for all of us.

The doorbell rang and I quickly answered it, smiling at Kane as he walked inside.

"Hello there. I'm here to pick up the dynamic duo for school."

"Uncle Kane!" both girls said at the same time, and I raised a brow.

"Uncle?" I whispered.

"Well, I'm Nora's uncle, and I think Lucy just caught on. It's not a hint or anything." He met my gaze. "Unless you need it to be a hint. You know, with Daisy. Because I can make that a hint. With my fist."

Kane grinned as Lake waddled up behind him.

"Excuse me, may I use your restroom?" she asked, and I moved out of her way, knowing that Lake could take me down in an instant. I might be trained, but I did not stand between a pregnant woman and the restroom.

"Thank you," she said, waving at the girls before she made her way to the restroom right down the hall.

I met Kane's gaze who once again shrugged.

"She can't fit behind the steering wheel and needed to get into her downtown office today. I'm going to drop her off after I drop the kids off."

"Nick still out of town?" I asked.

"Who knew they had tattoo conventions? But it brings in more money, and he's winning an award."

"I like Nick. He's pretty," Lucy said, and I pinched the bridge of my nose.

"No. I didn't hear that."

"Well, he is pretty," Kane said deadpan as Lake came out of the restroom.

"My husband is pretty. And so are you two. You guys all ready for school? Got your backpacks?"

I looked over at Lake and grinned. "You getting ready for that mom thing?"

"It seems like I'm forever waiting." She put her hands

on her very swollen belly and just sighed that happy pregnant sigh. I knew she was probably uncomfortable, tired, and anxious, but she looked happy.

My ex and I had never been like that. Everything had been awkward. Now though, I couldn't help but wonder what Daisy would look like pregnant.

And that was moving things a little too fast. I needed to tell her what I felt first. And I would. As soon as I got all of these people out of my house.

"Oh, we need to get one more thing," Lucy said, before she grabbed Nora's hand and they ran off to the back.

"Do not be late!" I called out.

"We won't!" Lucy answered.

"They're seriously the cutest," Lake said.

"Don't worry, I'll get them there on time," Kane added.

"Just don't drive like a bat out of hell to get there," I grumbled.

"Lucy and Nora are safe with me. I promise."

With the seriousness in his tone, I nodded right back. "I know. You wouldn't be here picking up my kid if I didn't trust you."

My phone rang again, and I looked down at the readout, smiling at Daisy's face.

"Hey, look who's calling."

"Oh, tell her hi for me. And I need all the tea," Lake said, and I rolled my eyes as I answered.

"Hey, babe. I'm headed into the office soon. You there now?"

Only Daisy didn't answer. There was a shout, a scuffle, the sound of flesh against flesh, and then a scream.

"Daisy? Daisy!"

I looked at Kane, whose face had hardened as he pulled out his phone.

Then I looked over at Lake, my hands fisting.

"Can you take care of the girls? Keep them here. They don't need to go to school. I don't know. Fuck."

Lake had her phone out, and I didn't know who she was calling, but I had a feeling it had to do with the Montgomery phone tree.

"You have the same security system as my house?" she asked, and I looked at Kane who nodded as he spoke rapidly to Ford on the other line.

"Lock them in. Keep them safe."

I looked up the stairs to where my daughter was, but I had to go. Daisy was hurt. She called and she was hurt and we needed to find her.

"I'll keep them safe."

"Ford's on his way over," Kane said as he ended the call and started another. "Stay here, Lake. Keep the kids safe. We're going to go get Daisy."

And then I was running out the door and into Kane's car, leaving mine behind.

I had the keys on the front table so if Lake needed to get out of there she could, but all I could think about was getting Daisy. My daughter was safe. Locked behind the security system and at home. Lake would keep her calm until I could talk to her.

I needed to find Daisy.

Kane drove like a bat out of hell, going far past the speed limit, and I prayed we didn't get pulled over.

"Daisy," I growled into the phone as I called again, but it kept going straight to voicemail.

"Somebody turned her fucking phone off," I spat.

"Noah's on the line," Kane said, his voice so cool that I knew that he was in the zone. He couldn't panic. Just like I couldn't. Kane wanted to kick ass. Just like I did.

"They turned off her phone, location services are off. Kingston's at the place now, and we called the cops. There's blood in the back, but there's not a lot, just some splatter. Kingston thinks it's from whoever attacked her, and maybe a little of hers as well. Her phone's still there, so is her purse. In her car. Fuck. Whatever device they used, scrambled our cameras."

I fisted my hand on the oh-shit bar, holding on tight as Kane skidded around a corner.

"Just like the cameras were scrambled at the warehouse? And at those other two places this week?"

Noah was silent, but I knew his mind was going in a thousand different directions, like mine. And then he cursed.

"Fuck. Okay. Cops are dealing with it, but so are we."

"They're not going to be able to find her as fast as we can. Find her, Noah."

"I'm on it."

"The location services on her phone are off. How the hell do you find her?"

"I have my ways. Her phone might not be on her, but all of you have your panic button on you at all times. Hers is on her belt. As long as she has her belt on, and didn't forget it at home, I can find her."

Noah hung up and I looked at Kane, my hands shaking. "We have to find her."

"We will. We're going to fucking find her."

"There's no other choice."

We drove in silence, and I knew I'd burn down the world for her.

"Those notes. Whoever left those notes. It was a warning. A threat."

"We all knew that. But the guy took enough time between notes and we did all we could do."

I looked at Kane as we took the exit. "Are you telling me that, or yourself?"

"I don't fucking know at this point. Daisy's family.

And I know you fucking love her. We're not going to let anything else happen to her."

I nodded as the phone rang and Kane answered on the car's Bluetooth.

"What?"

"I've got her. She's on Franklin Street, the warehouse next to the one that exploded."

My mind whirled as I tried to keep up.

"Who owns it?" I asked, my voice low.

"Walker Sellman."

From the way Noah bit out the name, his voice icy, I knew this man was going to be a dead man if any of us had anything to do with it.

"Walker Sellman. The same man that was fired for sexual harassment?"

"The same man who went to Sherman Priority Security," Kane added through gritted teeth.

"Get to the warehouse. The others are on their way. Don't be stupid. The authorities are on their way, too. Just get inside."

"Won't that be breaking and entering?" Kane asked, and I knew he didn't give a fuck. We were just covering our bases.

"I'll handle it with the cops. Just get the fuck inside. Get to Daisy."

I entered the address in the GPS, and then Kane was flying, though I didn't think the other man needed GPS.

None of them were going to forget where Daisy had almost died, where Kingston had watched his cousin nearly get blown up. We still talked about it; Daisy still had a limp when she was tired.

I was going to find her.

I wasn't going to let her get hurt.

Not ever again.

Chapter Eighteen

Daisy

"Wake up. Wake the fuck up. If you don't wake up, I'm going to make you wake up."

I dragged my eyes open, my mouth tasting like cardboard.

Of course, as soon as I opened my eyes, light slammed into them, blinding me, and I shut them again.

"Bitch!"

The slap across my face shouldn't have been surprising, but it still sent a shockwave through my system and I tasted blood in my mouth.

I tried to get a better sense of my surroundings. I was trained for this. I would be fine. Everything would be fine.

But the taser had hit me hard and my mouth hurt, my body ached, and while I didn't think I had broken a rib, the kidney shot had hurt. Everything ached. I had a cut on my forehead and minor cuts and bruises along my arms and sides. Someone had tied my arms in front of me. That was good. I could use that. They'd also tied my ankles together and taken my purse. My phone was gone, and I couldn't remember if I had made a call out or not.

But there were cameras, and people were waiting for me.

They would come for me.

I just had to be smart enough to be okay until they got here.

They would come for me, and then I would kick whoever's ass this was. Because I was fucking tired. So damn tired.

"Bitch," he mumbled again.

"Don't you know another word?" I lashed out, knowing that I probably shouldn't, but I didn't care.

Because I knew that voice. And everything started to click into place.

I finally opened my eyes and looked into the face of Walker Sellman.

A boring ass name for a boring ass man who didn't fucking care about anyone but himself.

This was the guy who owned the warehouse that had blown up.

This was the guy who we fired because he couldn't stop trying to rub himself on Jennifer and me and kept asking us to go to bed with him.

I hated him with everything that I was.

"Post-its? You threatened me with Post-its."

I was reaching here, but from the way his eyes narrowed, I had hit it right on the mark.

This man had been threatening me at my home and place of business. I had no idea what I'd done to deserve this kind of harassment.

"You've ruined me. Ruined me."

I looked at him in confusion. "What? What the hell are you talking about?"

"You weren't supposed to be in the fucking building when it exploded. I needed it for the insurance money. Then you fired me as a client, and due to the rumors, no one else would take me on."

"You did it on purpose? You set your own building on fire on purpose?"

"It was supposed to look like faulty wiring. And it would've worked except that you shouldn't have been there at the time. You were too fucking early." The man began to pace, the gun in his hand glinting under the lights.

I swallowed, knowing that if I wasn't careful, he was going to use it. This man was clearly on the brink, and I shouldn't push him. But I wanted to know everything because I was going to get out of this, and this man was going to jail for a very long time—after I kicked his ass.

I just needed Hugh and the others to get here.

Hugh.

He had to come, just like the others.

I trusted them all with everything that I was.

"Why? Was all of this worth it?"

"I didn't want you dead, I just wanted your company blamed for the attack. It's what Sherman's Priority Security wanted. We worked well together. They helped me set it up, and then they would take over your businesses. They're good at setting traps."

I thought of all the exhausting issues we'd had all week, and set that aside for now.

We would handle Sherman's Priority Security when the time came. But for now, I needed to get through this.

"But why? It just doesn't make sense to me. How is this worth it? How is taking me worth it?"

"Because you keep thriving. Nobody says no to me. But *you* did. Now you're going to learn what happens when you say no."

He grinned and ice slid down my spine.

No. I would not let him. He would not touch me.

"You'll learn. You'll finally learn," he spat.

"Walker, get on with it. If you're going to take her, just do it. We've got to get out of here."

"I've been waiting for this. You wouldn't let me have her before," Walker spat.

Three other guys walked in, and I recognized them now, as working for Sherman.

I could not believe that they had taken this drastic step. It didn't make any sense, but then again, not everybody was a good person.

They carried no guilt for hurting me, for blowing up a fucking building for insurance money.

That was when I realized they didn't care if they killed me.

"What are you going to do with her?" the lead man asked, and he didn't even look at me. There was nothing in his voice, nothing at all.

I couldn't move, not with all of them armed, but I'd find a way out.

"We'll move. But I'm taking her with me."

The security guy snorted.

"No. We're going to leave her here. Maybe this time she'll actually fucking die in the explosion."

I froze as I looked at the other man and all I saw there was death.

"It would've been easier if you'd just died the first time. But second time's the charm. You'll die in this building like you should have before, and the Montgomerys aren't going to be on our turf any longer. And I won't have to fucking deal with you and all of your damn morals."

"That wasn't the deal. She was supposed to be mine."

"You can have whatever cunt you want. Take that, and then we'll get you better cunt. But we're getting the fuck out of here."

The man snarled, and the three security guys left, leaving me alone with Walker.

"They've been lying to you. They're not working with you, they're just using you. Come on, let's get out of here. Please."

I heard the pleading in my voice and I didn't care. I was trying to remain calm, but we had to get out of there.

"Not until I'm done," Walker snapped, but I saw the hesitancy in his gaze.

"Please. Let's just get out of here."

"No. Because it's over for you. I'm going to get the money I've earned, and then I'm going to start my new company without dealing with all this shit. You guys almost bankrupted me before, and I'm not going to let it happen again. But first, I'm going to take what I deserve."

He came forward and I kicked out, tripping him and knocking my chair over. I crawled awkwardly, still tied up, cursing the knots that these guys had used.

I kept inching my way towards the door as Walker grabbed my thigh and squeezed, pulling me back. I kicked out again, using my bound hands to punch Walker in the nose. He cursed and reached for me, but I kept fighting.

Until gunshots echoed throughout the hall.

Adrenaline spiking, I looked towards the hallway, praying that nobody I loved was hurt.

We needed to get out of here. I couldn't let Hugh and the others get hurt.

They didn't know this place was rigged to blow.

Only, my attention was on the door and I hadn't paid attention to Walker. He pulled at me again, tugging at my belt, so I kneed him in the dick, slamming my forehead against his. The pain radiated through my head but I ignored it. They shouldn't have tied my arms in front of me, because I was stronger than him, even like this. And from the panic in his eyes, he knew it.

I got him to the ground and leaned over him, slamming my fists down on his face until he stopped fighting back.

He was still breathing, but unconscious, blood pooling between us.

Most of the blood was from his broken nose.

I turned him on his side so he wouldn't choke. I heard the shouts come closer but I had no idea who was coming—if they were an enemy or someone I cared about—so I kept inching my way towards the door, tears and blood dripping down my face.

I just needed to get out of here.

And then Hugh was there, running through the doorway. I heard my family calling out orders behind him.

My body began to shake as he untied me.

Kane was right behind him, gun drawn as he took in the surroundings then ran towards Walker.

"Don't kill him," I rasped. "Too much paperwork," I joked, and then I was free, and Hugh was holding me. I leaned into him, nuzzling my face into his neck.

He smelled so good, so much like home.

And I just wanted to go home.

"Daisy, baby."

"Hey, London boy," I rasped, and he let out a rough chuckle, holding me tighter.

"We have to go," I whispered, panic edging into my voice.

"We will. We will. The cops are on their way. Noah says it's handled, but we're going to have some explaining to do."

I shook my head quickly. "No. They rigged this place to blow like they did the other one. We have to go *now*."

Hugh cursed and looked over my head.

I was so exhausted that I barely heard him and Kane shouting at one another, and then I was in Hugh's arms and we were running out of the building, Kane cursing about dead weight over his shoulder behind us.

So we weren't leaving Walker to die.

More's the pity.

We ran out of the building as the cops showed up, Noah with them.

Thank God for Noah, who could sweet-talk anyone.

Ford was there, as was his eldest brother for some reason.

"Ford's brothers own the other buildings, long story, but they're here to help."

"We have to tell them."

"Already on it. We're on comms."

I nodded and looked up at him as the EMTs came toward us.

"We have to hurry."

"Bomb squad's on the way. We're safe. I promise you. You're safe."

I just shook my head in his arms and looked him dead in the eyes.

"I love you. I was going to tell you before this. But I fucking love you."

He smiled at me, my ginger haired London boy, looking so beautiful, disheveled, and all mine.

"I was going to tell you tonight. I love you, baby. We're going to make this work. You and me. But I swear to God, no more buildings like this."

I was crying when he kissed me, and I ignored the sting in my lips from the cut, and just let him hold me.

And I only had eyes for Hugh as my family milled about, as Ford's family joined us, and we dealt with the aftermath.

I didn't know what was going to happen, I didn't know who we would have to talk to next, but I held the man I loved and knew there was no going back.

I had fallen in love long before this, now I'd finally found the courage to say it.

"I love you," I whispered.

"I love you, too," he whispered right back.

"You guys know you're still on comms, right?" Kingston asked, sounding annoyed and relieved at the same time.

"Seriously. Don't do anything else that I don't want to hear," Kane rumbled.

"I'm just glad the cat is finally out of the bag. But get off comms," Noah ordered, and I laughed, not realizing I could.

"Well, good to know your family approves."

"Oh, they weren't going to have a choice," I teased.

"There's always a choice," Kingston corrected.

I shut off comms and kissed Hugh again as the paramedics worked around him.

"I have no idea how we're going to explain this to Lucy, not the loving you part, I think she figured that out before both of us," Hugh added, and I laughed. "But this whole thing. We'll figure it out. One day at a time."

I cupped his face, and sighed, finally feeling somewhat relaxed for the first time in weeks.

"One day at a time."

He kissed me again and I sighed, ignoring the looks from my family as they all groaned, because we might not be on comms, but they all knew anyway.

Exactly how I wanted it.

Chapter Nineteen

Daisy

"What part of immediate family only for this dinner did you not understand?" I asked, only teasing. And because they knew I was teasing, both Kane and Kingston hugged me tight and kissed my cheeks.

"We might not be part of this nuclear family, but we are still family. We heard there would be food. I mean, really, we're here for the food." Kingston winked at me, but Kane looked shadowed. Sad. Frankly, I didn't blame him. I wasn't okay. Physically I would be, but it was going to take a while for us to be okay again.

"Kane?" I asked, my voice low.

"I'm fine. Really. But you really think we're going to let you out of our sight right now? I mean, come on. You know the rules. You don't get to leave us anytime soon. You got me?"

I held up my hands in surrender. "Fine, I understand. But you get to explain to my mother."

"Explain to your mother what?" Mom asked as she came over, a bright smile on her face. Probably a little too bright. Of course, I didn't blame her. I had been beyond scared. Even though I knew I could handle myself, even though I knew my team and the love of my life would be there, I had been scared. My mom had almost lost her daughter. So no, I wasn't going to blame her for not wanting me out of her sight anytime soon. Just like Kane and Kingston.

"They're just here for free food."

My mom narrowed her gaze at them before she winked. "Of course, you're welcome here boys. Free food all around. I'm just surprised the rest of your crew isn't here. I know the entire Montgomery Inc. Security branch likes to hang out. It's funny, our generation liked to be split up by cousins, because we all lived in different cities, but because we've blended so much, you guys tend to hang out by teams. I never really thought about it that way."

I shrugged, leaning against my mom. "It makes sense. We work together, and though we all live in different neighborhoods, we hang out."

"Noah and Sebastian would be here, but they are at Greer's brother's house for her family dinner. Apparently there are other families out there."

"You say that as if you don't hang out with your dad's side of the family often," I teased. "Just like I do."

Kane smiled then, his eyes warming just a little.

"That is true. Plus, you know Greer has three hot brothers. Wonder if they're single." He tapped his chin and Kingston rolled his eyes.

"Really? Because we both know you're not going to be looking towards that set of friends of the family. You have another one on your mind."

Confused, I looked between them. "What? What did I miss?"

"Nothing," Kane grumbled.

"No, I have questions. A lot of questions. You're seeing someone? Why didn't I know? I should be the first one to know these things!"

"And you call yourself a security specialist," Kingston teased.

"I need to know these things."

"No, you don't. Let them have some privacy. Just like they gave you and Hugh some privacy."

I scowled at my mother. "They did not. None of you did. You all are just as curious and invasive with my relationships as I am with theirs. It's what we do as a family."

"Be a good girl and go sit down. I don't want you standing up, especially when you're still bruised."

"Listen to your mother," Kingston said solemnly, and I shoved at his shoulder.

"Jerk."

"It's like you have thirty brothers rather than just one sister. I like it. But I swear, keep your hands to yourselves, children," my mom warned, and I sighed.

"Yes, Mom."

"Yes, Aunt Adrienne," Kingston grumbled.

My mom laughed and went to talk to my dad, who was in the kitchen cooking with Amy. My sister looked up from the kitchen island and gave me a soft smile. I waved. She wasn't great at seeing me hurt. Hell, nobody was. I had scared my family, something I tried not to do, but I tended to keep doing it. I loved my job. I loved keeping people safe. But the company had nearly broken us. I still couldn't believe that Sherman Priority Security decided that they were going to take out their revenge on me personally.

And Walker Sellman, the owner of that building,

hated me. And wanted me. And it had turned into this twisted and sadistic obsession.

He hadn't liked that we'd fired him. Hadn't liked that when he'd sexually harassed us, Jennifer and I had pushed him away. And for some reason, I had been his target.

So he had done his best to find me, to hurt me, and to scare me.

Well, it had worked. Scared me to the point that I tried not to think about it.

And I had been scared. So damn scared. I had almost lost everything important to me.

We weren't done yet; there were still loose ends when it came to Sherman Priority Security. But the authorities were working on it, and honestly, I had to trust them. I had to trust my team.

Because I had more important things to focus on.

It was as if I had summoned them with my mind.

"Daisy!" Lucy called out as she walked into the house. I hadn't heard the front door open or the doorbell, but my mother came behind them, her arm hooked with Hugh as they spoke quietly.

I opened my arms as Lucy ran towards me and skidded to a stop in front of me.

"Will I hurt you? I don't want to hurt you."

The fear in that little girl's voice nearly sent me over the edge, and I beckoned her towards me.

"Maybe don't jump on me, but snuggle with me? I'm really okay. I promise."

Lucy scrambled on the couch and sat next to me, pressing her cheek to my neck and holding me tight.

I loved this little girl. I loved her and I wanted to be in her life. She was so damn special, so full of sparkles and energy and everything good.

I had scared her. And that was something Hugh and I were going to have to deal with. Because I loved him. Just like I loved this little girl. I wanted to be part of their lives. And while we were still taking our time, figuring out who we were and making sure we didn't move too quickly, I felt good with her in my arms and Hugh looking at us as if we were his whole world.

And perhaps we were.

"How was dance rehearsal?" I asked, sliding my hands through Lucy's hair. She pulled back and grinned. "So much fun. Nora is teaching me everything she knows. I'm so glad she's one of my best friends. And I can have more best friends and not just her, but she's special. Plus, I like that she's part of your family. So it's like I am too." She ducked her head, blushing as she said it, and I swallowed the lump in my throat before hugging her close and kissing the top of her head.

"That is the sweetest thing. And you're right, she is part of my family. And you are too." I looked up at Hugh, who still had his arm around my mom. He smiled at me, the love in his eyes not surprising, but it still felt so new. I never expected this. This life of mine.

I knew what it was like to be loved. To be chosen. My family had chosen me. They showed me in every moment of every day what it felt like to be loved. So I believed in love. I believed in happy ever afters and happiness and choice and romance and all of that.

But it had also felt as if I was never going to find it. That I would always be standing behind and watching as those I loved found love. I could never hate them for it, I just wanted it as well.

I had gone on date after date, had met man after man who I thought had truly seen me. But they had only seen what they wanted to see. They saw a woman they thought they could handle. But they couldn't handle my strength, my tenacity, my bullheadedness. They couldn't handle the fact that I was the boss. That I could kick their ass and save the day if I needed to.

And then Hugh had come along.

The man I could save, just like he could save me. Hugh would be there to help me stand on my own.

I didn't have to ask, he was just there.

And I was fine with how I fit into his life. Because he was it.

He was the answer to the question I never let myself ask.

He was my last first kiss.

And wasn't that something to think about?

My mom said something, but I was listening to Lucy telling me about her day, while Kane and Kingston went into the kitchen to help.

Hugh came to sit next to me and I looked at him over my shoulder and grinned.

"Sorry I couldn't make it to dance."

"I'm glad you are resting." He kissed me softly, and I fell in love with him all over again. I loved this man.

I was honestly still so surprised this was mine.

"Can I have a kiss too, Daddy?" Lucy asked, and he leaned over me and kissed his daughter's cheek.

"Is that good?"

"That's perfect. And, Daisy? Can I have one too?" She sounded so sweet and innocent, I knew she was going to be a handful. I couldn't wait. I kissed her other cheek, then tickled her, loving the way she laughed.

"Oh, Lucy, I might have a treat for you," my dad called out, and she wiggled off the couch.

"You promise you'll be here when I get back? You won't leave?"

Hugh stiffened at my side and everyone in the kitchen stopped what they were doing and watched the scene in front of them. Because all of them understood. Of course we did.

I nearly died and that had scared her. And she was still reeling from what happened with her mother. But I would be there. And I would prove that. Day in and day out. All with the man that I loved by my side.

I reached out and took Daisy's hand and squeezed. "I'll be right here. I promise. And tomorrow I'll be right where you need me. Okay?"

"I love you."

I heard my mother and my sister sniff. Even Kane cleared his throat as Kingston wiped his face.

I held out my arms and let Lucy sink into my hold.

"I love you so much, baby girl. I love you." I kissed her cheek as Hugh squeezed my shoulder, and then Lucy was running off, laughing it up as my dad told a joke and I watched my family embrace that little girl like she was their own.

Because she was.

"I should let you know that little girl has become a Montgomery. I'm sorry, she's now one of us. It's a cult. You'll get over it."

Hugh shook his head. "I had no idea what I was in for when I saw you at that wedding. But I'm pretty sure I'm okay with my daughter and I joining this cult. You guys have good cheese."

"That is part of our logo and letterhead."

"Do you think we should tell Rina and Henry how you and I met?" I asked, mentioning the friends of ours and their wedding that had started this all.

"Oh yes. They're going to want to know. I have a

feeling watching you walk in as my boss will be the hottest thing."

I rolled my eyes. "Honestly. With most guys I would say that was a line. And yet you? I'm a little worried it's true."

"Oh yes. Completely true. I have a thing. Are you really feeling okay?" he asked softly, and I leaned forward, pressing my forehead to his. This felt so right.

"I'm feeling better. Tired. But that's what happens when you pass out after being tased."

He scowled and I patted his chest. "I'm really fine. I promise. And that does mean I'd really like to make sure you know exactly how fine I feel later." I did my best to add a suggestive tone, even though we were surrounded by my family.

Hugh kissed me softly.

"I think that can be arranged."

"What can be arranged?" Kingston asked as he came bounding in, Lucy on his back.

"A cheese plate. A cheese plate can be arranged," I lied, and Kane just rolled his eyes as Lucy grinned.

"We have cheese. Your mom and dad love cheese. And I think I do too."

"That's my girl," Kingston said proudly.

I shook my head at Hugh. "I'm sorry. She's now one of us."

"I don't mind. I think she's in good hands. And, well, I like cheese."

"But clotted cream is gross," Kane added, setting the cheeseboard down on the table in front of us.

"Then you haven't had good clotted cream. Don't worry, I'll teach you all. And how to brew tea. Because the fact that you Americans use a microwave...I can't." He shuddered.

"I'll have you know we have an electric kettle; I know how to brew tea." I scowled at him.

"Oh really? I guess you'll have to show me."

"Okay, enough of that," Kane said. "What do you say? Do you want a Gouda, or Havarti?" he asked Lucy, who tapped her mouth with her little finger and looked so serious, I couldn't help but smile.

"You don't have to choose. You can try both, I promise."

I was so blessed to have her in my life. To be in her life. I just needed to make sure that no matter what, I would always be worthy of her.

"Really? I don't have to choose?"

"Never," my sister said as she hugged Lucy. "You're one of us now. There's cheese for all."

"Cheese for all," the Montgomerys said as one. Hugh looked at me, a little panic in his gaze.

"Worried yet? Ready to run?" I asked, only partially teasing.

Hugh went serious before he kissed my cheek. "Never. I'm all in."

"Same."

I mouthed the words "I love you," and he repeated them back. We laughed with my family over cheese, and I sank into the arms of the man I loved, and knew the choices we made had led us here, no matter how confusing.

He had been a man across the aisle, a man that was only supposed to be a one-night stand.

And then he had turned into more. So much more.

I trusted him with my heart, my body, my mind, my future.

I trusted him with me.

And he was mine. On the first day, on the last, and every day and kiss in between.

Chapter Twenty

Kane

It had been the week of all weeks, the year of all years. Not that I was ever going to say that out loud—that was just asking for trouble. I wasn't usually one to believe in fate or luck, especially not with the year I'd been having, however maybe there was a way to get through the next few weeks. And forget about the fact that things kept getting in my way. And making things even more difficult.

I still couldn't believe everything that had happened. Or the fact that we still didn't have answers. I'd almost lost one of my best friends all because of someone's ego.

That was rich coming from me, because yes, we Montgomerys had egos. Though I wasn't a Montgomery by last name.

I had my dad's last name, and a big family without even adding in the Montgomerys. My aunts all had huge families, and my dad just happened to marry a Montgomery. So I had Montgomery in my middle name, just like many other cousins. I wasn't sure which of my aunts and uncles had decided to make that a thing, but apparently the Montgomery name would not die.

"What's going on?" Kingston asked from where he stood next to me, a frown on his face.

I shook my head.

"Nothing's wrong."

"That sounds like a lie," Kingston said with a laugh. We were the closest cousins in our business. Kingston and I were close in age, and though technically we were second cousins, two offshoots of the family trees, we acted more like brothers than anything. Which meant Kingston could read my mind when I didn't want him to. The damn man.

"So, you're not going to talk about it," Kingston paused, "Her?"

I whirled on him, narrowing my gaze. "No, we're not. You know we're not. You know *why* we're not."

"The thing is, I don't. I don't know why you're acting this way. I don't know why you won't talk about her. Or the fact that some really huge fucking things happened and you're not talking about them, either."

"What am I supposed to talk about? It didn't work out. But Daisy's safe. What else is there? Our family's safe. Our work is good. Business is up. I don't want to talk about it. Okay?"

"If you didn't sound so defensive about it, maybe I would believe you."

"Maybe it's not up for you to believe me. Just go. I'm going to close up shop and head out."

"You can talk to me, you know. You can talk to any of us. You don't have to keep it inside anymore."

I glared at him. "That's pretty rich coming from you."

Kingston shut up, his eyes going cold.

"You're an asshole sometimes, you know."

"Right back at you."

He huffed and grabbed his phone from his desk.

"Come to the bar with us. We should just stop hiding shit."

"I'm fine. I promise."

Kingston gave me one last look before he headed out, locking the front door behind him. I'd go out the back way, ensuring everything was locked up tight, the security cameras were going, and had the alarm on. We were all set to go.

So why did I have a tingle on the back of my neck?

Maybe because we still hadn't found one last guy. The cops were looking for him, but he was long gone. He'd taken his money and run off. We all knew that. But I still had an uneasy feeling.

I grabbed my things, did one last check around the building, and made my way out to the back parking lot where the employees parked. It was dark outside, but we had enough lights going so there were no shadows to hide in. Considering we not only owned the building, but each of the businesses inside were owned by our family, why the hell would we risk their safety? After all, we'd had enough happen to us recently, enough horror and terror, that we amped up our own security. It was our job to protect our family. And we had failed more often than not. But never again.

"Montgomery."

I froze at the familiar voice, even though it wasn't my name, and turned.

I knew that face, knew that voice. And hadn't expected to see it here.

"What do you think you're going to accomplish here?" I asked, my hands still in my pockets. I did my best to try to dial my phone without making it look like I was, but the man's gaze narrowed, his finger tightening on the trigger.

Fuck.

"Hands out of your fucking pockets."

I slowly did as he asked, cursing under my breath for letting Kingston go by himself. But at least he wasn't here for this. I'd talk my way out of this, just like I talked my way out of everything. But why hadn't we seen him coming? I looked up and saw the knocked-out security camera. Fuck. Well, the man was fast. And good.

But I was better.

"Let's just talk this out."

"Fuck you, Montgomery."

"Kane?" a soft voice asked, and the blood in my veins froze, my entire body going on alert.

"Phoebe, get out!" I called.

The man turned towards her, whirling with the gun in his hand. I didn't think twice, I just moved, throwing myself towards Phoebe as her eyes widened at the sight of the man behind the dumpster, gun raised, and I knew fate was laughing at me for thinking it didn't exist.

Because it did. It always did.

She looked at me and I saw the confusion and terror in her gaze. I saw everything I hadn't been able to before.

Because she was the woman I loved. The woman that wasn't mine. And I threw myself on top of her, and when the gun went off, she screamed.

If you'd like to read a bonus scene from Daisy & Hugh: Check out this special Epilogue!

NEXT IN THE MONTGOMERY INK LEGACY SERIES:

Kane and Phoebe make things...interesting in HIS SECOND CHANCE.

Bonus Epilogue

Hugh

I leaned back in the chair, listening as the waves hit the sand over and over again, the melodic and methodic echoing lulling me to sleep. We were on day four of our vacation, and it was perfect. I wasn't usually a beach person. I lived in one of the sunniest places in North America, at least when it came to continuous days of sun. I was covered in sunblock, wearing a hat, and about to scooch under the umbrella to the right of me.

"You look so adorable covered in sunscreen."

"I'm wearing the reef-safe stuff, and about to go hide under the shade." I looked at Daisy as she walked towards me, the black bikini making my mouth water.

"I like that you're protecting your skin."

"You tan nicely, even with the amount of sunscreen and shirts that you wear to keep yourself protected. Me? I look like a tomato. A crispy one."

Daisy bent down and slid her lips over mine. We were in a private cabana, so I slid my hand down her thigh and squeezed. My eyes were open, so all I could do was look down at her beautiful breasts that were just begging for my attention.

"Come over here and sit on me. Protect me from the sun."

Daisy laughed before shaking her head at me. "Well, that's a line if I've ever heard one."

"What? I don't want to get sunburned. You could protect me."

"Really? You're afraid your dick is going to get sunburned?"

I winced. "Dear God. That sounds extremely painful."

"You're right, that does sound painful. Don't worry, I'll protect you."

She bent down again, kissed me, and, to my disappointment, took my hand to pull me up off the chair.

"Come on, there's a bed with our name on it."

"You're no fun," I growled, but I followed her to the bed on the side of the beach.

We weren't going to our bedroom, one where we had made love countless times since we arrived. No, this one was underneath the canopy, and still private. This was one of the exclusive resorts owned by a friend of her family. Seriously, the number of connections the Montgomerys had was a little insane. But I did not mind those connections. Because now I could have sex with the woman that I loved right on the beach, and no one was going to say a thing.

That made me grin, as we toppled onto the bed, safe under the shade.

"Show me where you're sunburned," she teased as she slid over me.

We were still in our bathing suits, and I slid my hands up and down her thighs.

"Kiss and make it better?" I moved one hand to the back of her neck and pulled her down to me. She sank over me, the warmth of her pussy pressed against my cock. I was already peeking out of the top of my shorts, and I knew I wasn't going to last long in this position, not when she was just so warm. She tasted of the pina coladas we had earlier, and I grinned, deepening the kiss. When she raked her fingernails down my chest, I winced.

"Are you okay?"

"Sadly, I did get a slight sunburn."

She tsked before leaning down to kiss over my skin.

"Feel better?"

I slid my hands into her hair, gesturing her for a kiss

lower. She rolled her eyes but moved down. She slid my cock out of my swim trunks, and I groaned as she slowly began to lick up and down the shaft.

"Oh, I think that helps."

She laughed against my dick, humming along the length. I lay back, enjoying the attention, knowing this was one of the best ways to enjoy our afternoon.

I still couldn't believe that this was my fate. That I was so damn lucky to have this woman as mine.

She hollowed her mouth, nearly sending me over the edge with that one action.

"Dear God," I growled as I tugged on her hair.

She sighed and pouted at me.

"Seriously? You're not going to let me finish?"

"Nope. I'm going to need you to come over here and let me have you."

"Lazy," she mumbled, before she reached up to undo her top. Her breasts fell heavy into my hands. I rolled her nipples between my fingers and she closed her eyes, sliding her hips up and down my body.

"Witch," I growled, forcing myself not to come on my stomach with that motion. She was so damn beautiful, so damn hot. It was hard to think when I was around her. But that had always been the case. From that first dance until this moment, she had been on my mind, and would be until the end of our days. I was so damn lucky she was mine, and I was never going to forget this. She was mine and I was hers, and I wanted her. We rolled so she was beneath me, and I sucked and licked at her nipples until they were bright cherries.

"So beautiful. I love that your nipples are so sensitive." She rubbed her legs together beneath me before I slid my body between her legs, not letting her move. Not letting her come without me.

"Tease."

I smiled against her lips, kissing her softly.

"You're so beautiful," I whispered before I undid the ties of her suit, tossing it over my shoulder.

She spread her legs for me as I bent between them, having my fill. Her hands were on her breasts as she rocked her hips on my face. I licked and sucked. She tasted of sweet honey. I loved eating her out, loved tasting every inch of her. Her skin was so soft, so delicate, and it reddened from my touch.

I wanted her, loved her, and she was all mine. When she came, her honey flowing on my tongue, I lapped up every morsel, every ounce, because she was mine.

I finally leaned back as she lay spent beneath me, and tugged off my shorts. I hovered over her, and when she pulled me down to her; I entered her swift and hard.

"Hugh," she whispered.

"Daisy. My Daisy."

And we made love as the breeze slid over our skin, and did our best to keep quiet, knowing that while others couldn't see us, our voices could echo over the waves.

She arched for me, her pussy clamping around my cock, her orgasm so beautiful. I rolled to my back, letting her ride me, my hands on her breasts. It was all I could do not to come right away, but I told myself to hold back, to breathe.

And then she was on all fours, crawling to the headboard and holding on, and I was pounding into her from behind, my hands on her breasts.

When I finally came, filling her up, we shook, collapsing in a heap on the tangled linen.

Our breaths coming in pants, we both ached, shaking.

"What round was that?" she asked, clearly out of breath.

I laughed, still hard inside her as I kissed her bare shoulder.

"I quit counting a couple of days ago."

Her body shook as she laughed and I held her close, pulling the sheets over us.

"We should probably get dressed; I know our lunch should be arriving soon. And while they knock, we don't need to show anyone my ass."

"But it's a beautiful ass."

"And I'm a ginger, I don't need it sunburned."

We slid out of bed, laughing, covered ourselves in

sheets, and made our way to the shower. We made love again, and we took our time, enjoying each other.

After, I got dressed in board shorts, while she wore a sundress, neither of us bothering with underwear. We'd touch each other again soon. It was so odd, this feeling, this need. But it was all I could do not to want more.

"Are you ready to call Lucy?" she asked, and I nodded, pulling out my phone. Lunch had been delivered, and while we were snacking on a charcuterie board, because my Montgomery loved her cheese, and a few other local delights from the island, I looked at the time.

"I'm glad your parents are watching her. While I want to take Lucy with us on as many trips as possible, I am going to sometimes be selfish with you."

She sat next to me on the oversized chair and snuggled into my side.

"Same. I love Lucy. I'm so grateful that she's in our lives. But I'm also really excited that we had this trip."

"You're right. I fucking love you." I kissed the top of her head as I pressed call.

Daisy's mom answered with a bright laugh as Lucy jumped into her new grandmother's lap and waved.

"Daisy! Dad!"

"There's my little girl," I said, my heart feeling two sizes too big.

"Hey, Lucy girl," Daisy said, waving back.

The relationship between my daughter and Daisy

was nothing I had ever expected. Lucy's mother had yet to call or reach out at all. She had cut off all ties, and I knew the next step would be to get the paperwork signed for her to permanently sever all parental ties. It was what Lucy's birth mom wanted, and now, after seeing the way Daisy was around Lucy, I knew it would be for the best. My ex had offered, had wanted it, and I'd initially denied it, wanting to hope for my kid. But I was delusional. It was time to move on, and with what would happen next, I knew it was time.

"Yesterday and this morning we went snorkeling, and we saw a barracuda."

Lucy's eyes widened as Daisy's mom blinked.

"A barracuda? No, thank you."

"Is that the one with all the teeth?" Lucy asked, chomping her teeth together.

I snorted and nodded. "Yes, but we were a safe distance away. Don't worry, we're having fun."

"I'm having fun too. Grandma and Grandpa are showing me how to use my new drawing pad. I'm going to be a tattoo artist like them."

I saw the look on Adrienne Montgomery-Knight's face as Lucy called her "Grandma" and I nearly teared up.

It hadn't been a sudden thing, and we hadn't pushed it, but Lucy had found her family just like I had. And I knew to the end of my days I would remember this moment. The way Daisy and Lucy chatted a mile a minute, and the way Daisy's mother looked as if she had the whole world in her arms. This was her first grand-baby, and just like Adrienne had been brought into Daisy's life later on, Daisy was brought into Lucy's.

"And you're coming home soon? Because I miss you. Both of you." Lucy grinned big, and I nodded.

"We'll be home soon."

"And you're going to do the thing?" she asked as Adrienne narrowed her gaze and Daisy looked at me in confusion.

I grinned nervously and nodded. "Soon, I promise, baby."

"Okay, have fun, Daddy. And have fun, Daisy! I can't wait for you to be my mommy!" And with that, Lucy hung up without letting anyone else say goodbye.

I looked at the blank phone and burst out laughing, wondering how I got so lucky with my kid, even though she was the worst secret-keeper.

Daisy turned to look at me. "Did she just say mommy?"

"She might have. I swear, that kid."

"Hugh," she said, and I cleared my throat. I knew the perfectly laid-out dinner I had planned for later wasn't going to work. No, this was better.

I reached into my pants pocket and pulled out the ring.

It was a simple princess-cut diamond with black stones all around it.

"I had to ask Lucy if she was okay with this first. And if she wanted to be here for it. But she said she wanted you to have the perfect princess proposal. She's been watching too many movies with happy ever afters."

"Hugh," Daisy said, tears filling her eyes.

"Daisy Montgomery-Knight. There has always been a connection from the first moment I saw you, and I knew in that moment my life would change. I just didn't realize it would be like this. I love you more than anything I thought possible. You are my everything, *our* everything. You are a light in my daughter's life, just like you are in mine. When I asked Lucy if it was okay if I asked you to marry me and to be in her life, she was so excited she burst out crying, begging for you to be her mom. We wanted to keep it a surprise. She wanted this princess time for you, as she put it. So, be my princess? Marry me? Make me so damn happy and complete our family. What do you say, Daisy, will you marry me?"

I was rambling, my words coming quick. Daisy just looked at me, then down at the ring, before she threw her arms around me. I nearly dropped the ring before I clutched it in my fist and held her close.

"I take it that's a yes?" I asked.

"Yes. Always. Oh my God. Yes."

I kissed her and slid the ring on her finger.

"Perfect fit. You're so strong. The strongest most capable woman I know. And I know that I'm safe, that my daughter's safe, that my family's safe in your arms. But I'm so grateful that I can be your protector, too."

I kissed her again.

"Look at you, with the words to make me cry. You know I hate crying."

"Well, I had to make sure that when we recount this to Lucy, she would approve."

"And really that's all that matters," she said.

"I love you, Daisy."

"I love you too, Hugh. And I love Lucy too. And I'm so grateful that I get to help you with that baby girl. She called me mommy."

I wiped tears from her cheeks again and pressed my lips to her forehead.

"Our daughter. She's so loved. And with the number of family members she's about to have in her life? She's never going to question it again."

I held Daisy close and knew that we were going to have to call Lucy back and let her know that Daisy would be part of our lives forever.

I loved Daisy Montgomery-Knight. And I always would.

She was ours, our family. And I couldn't wait to take our next step. Together.

A Note from Carrie Ann Ryan

Thank you so much for reading **LAST FIRST KISS!**

This book came out of an idea of what would happen if you met your soulmate at a wedding and never planned on seeing him again. Then, of course, one of my audio besties asked me to write a book for her favorite narrator, Shane East, and Hugh was born!

This book touched my heart and I so loved writing Daisy and Hugh's romance. I knew when I started writing the next generation of Montgomerys, I'd write Daisy's. I just didn't realize how much FUN I'd have writing it!

Next time? Kane gets his story in His Second Chance. You've only had a glimpse of Phoebe but she has...well secrets. Mwah ah ah ah. This book will be a little twisty and I cannot WAIT.

BTW Greer's brothers get their own series called the First Time series. Heath will be book 1 in Good Time Boyfriend!! Three brothers. Three books. And all the emotional heat. Because the Cassidy brothers are moving to Denver and everything is about to change.

And as for Ford's brothers? Well....it won't be a secret for you because The Cage Brothers will begin soon. Make sure you're signed up for my newsletter so you know when you can hear more because keeping this series secret is SO HARD!

The Montgomery Ink Legacy Series:

Book 1: Bittersweet Promises
Book 2: At First Meet
Book 2.5: Happily Ever Never
Book 3: Longtime Crush
Book 4: Best Friend Temptation
Book 4.5: Happily Ever Maybe
Book 5: Last First Kiss
Book 6: His Second Chance
Book 7: One Night with You

If you'd like to read a bonus scene from Daisy & Hugh:

Check out this special Epilogue!

NEXT IN THE MONTGOMERY INK LEGACY SERIES:
Kane and Phoebe make things…interesting in HIS SECOND CHANCE.

If you want to make sure you know what's coming next from me, you can sign up for my newsletter at www.CarrieAnnRyan.com; follow me on twitter at @CarrieAnnRyan, or like my Facebook page. I also have a Facebook Fan Club where we have trivia, chats, and other goodies. You guys are the reason I get to do what I do and I thank you.

Make sure you're signed up for my MAILING LIST so you can know when the next releases are available as well as find giveaways and FREE READS.

Happy Reading!

Also from Carrie Ann Ryan

The Montgomery Ink Legacy Series:

Book 1: Bittersweet Promises

Book 2: At First Meet

Book 2.5: Happily Ever Never

Book 3: Longtime Crush

Book 4: Best Friend Temptation

Book 4.5: Happily Ever Maybe

Book 5: Last First Kiss

Book 6: His Second Chance

Book 7: One Night with You

The Wilder Brothers Series:

Book 1: One Way Back to Me

Book 2: Always the One for Me

Book 3: The Path to You

Book 4: Coming Home for Us
Book 5: Stay Here With Me
Book 6: Finding the Road to Us
Book 7: Moments for You
Book 7.5: A Wilder Wedding
Book 8: Forever For Us
Book 9: Pieces of Me

The Cage Family
Book 1: The Forever Rule

The First Time Series:
Book 1: Good Time Boyfriend
Book 2: Last Minute Fiancé
Book 3: Second Chance Husband

The Aspen Pack Series:
Book 1: Etched in Honor
Book 2: Hunted in Darkness
Book 3: Mated in Chaos
Book 4: Harbored in Silence
Book 5: Marked in Flames

The Montgomery Ink: Fort Collins Series:
Book 1: Inked Persuasion
Book 2: Inked Obsession
Book 3: Inked Devotion

Book 3.5: Nothing But Ink
Book 4: Inked Craving
Book 5: Inked Temptation

The Montgomery Ink: Boulder Series:

Book 1: Wrapped in Ink
Book 2: Sated in Ink
Book 3: Embraced in Ink
Book 3: Moments in Ink
Book 4: Seduced in Ink
Book 4.5: Captured in Ink
Book 4.7: Inked Fantasy
Book 4.8: A Very Montgomery Christmas

Montgomery Ink: Colorado Springs

Book 1: Fallen Ink
Book 2: Restless Ink
Book 2.5: Ashes to Ink
Book 3: Jagged Ink
Book 3.5: Ink by Numbers

Montgomery Ink Denver:

Book 0.5: Ink Inspired
Book 0.6: Ink Reunited
Book 1: Delicate Ink
Book 1.5: Forever Ink
Book 2: Tempting Boundaries

Book 3: Harder than Words
Book 3.5: Finally Found You
Book 4: Written in Ink
Book 4.5: Hidden Ink
Book 5: Ink Enduring
Book 6: Ink Exposed
Book 6.5: Adoring Ink
Book 6.6: Love, Honor, & Ink
Book 7: Inked Expressions
Book 7.3: Dropout
Book 7.5: Executive Ink
Book 8: Inked Memories
Book 8.5: Inked Nights
Book 8.7: Second Chance Ink
Book 8.5: Montgomery Midnight Kisses
Bonus: Inked Kingdom

The On My Own Series:

Book 0.5: My First Glance
Book 1: My One Night
Book 2: My Rebound
Book 3: My Next Play
Book 4: My Bad Decisions

The Promise Me Series:

Book 1: Forever Only Once
Book 2: From That Moment

Book 3: Far From Destined

Book 4: From Our First

The Less Than Series:

Book 1: Breathless With Her

Book 2: Reckless With You

Book 3: Shameless With Him

The Fractured Connections Series:

Book 1: Breaking Without You

Book 2: Shouldn't Have You

Book 3: Falling With You

Book 4: Taken With You

The Whiskey and Lies Series:

Book 1: Whiskey Secrets

Book 2: Whiskey Reveals

Book 3: Whiskey Undone

The Gallagher Brothers Series:

Book 1: Love Restored

Book 2: Passion Restored

Book 3: Hope Restored

The Ravenwood Coven Series:

Book 1: Dawn Unearthed

Book 2: Dusk Unveiled

Book 3: Evernight Unleashed

The Talon Pack:

Book 1: Tattered Loyalties
Book 2: An Alpha's Choice
Book 3: Mated in Mist
Book 4: Wolf Betrayed
Book 5: Fractured Silence
Book 6: Destiny Disgraced
Book 7: Eternal Mourning
Book 8: Strength Enduring
Book 9: Forever Broken
Book 10: Mated in Darkness
Book 11: Fated in Winter

Redwood Pack Series:

Book 1: An Alpha's Path
Book 2: A Taste for a Mate
Book 3: Trinity Bound
Book 3.5: A Night Away
Book 4: Enforcer's Redemption
Book 4.5: Blurred Expectations
Book 4.7: Forgiveness
Book 5: Shattered Emotions
Book 6: Hidden Destiny
Book 6.5: A Beta's Haven
Book 7: Fighting Fate

Book 7.5: Loving the Omega
Book 7.7: The Hunted Heart
Book 8: Wicked Wolf

The Elements of Five Series:

Book 1: From Breath and Ruin
Book 2: From Flame and Ash
Book 3: From Spirit and Binding
Book 4: From Shadow and Silence

Dante's Circle Series:

Book 1: Dust of My Wings
Book 2: Her Warriors' Three Wishes
Book 3: An Unlucky Moon
Book 3.5: His Choice
Book 4: Tangled Innocence
Book 5: Fierce Enchantment
Book 6: An Immortal's Song
Book 7: Prowled Darkness
Book 8: Dante's Circle Reborn

Holiday, Montana Series:

Book 1: Charmed Spirits
Book 2: Santa's Executive
Book 3: Finding Abigail
Book 4: Her Lucky Love
Book 5: Dreams of Ivory

The Branded Pack Series:

(Written with Alexandra Ivy)

Book 1: Stolen and Forgiven

Book 2: Abandoned and Unseen

Book 3: Buried and Shadowed

About the Author

Carrie Ann Ryan is the New York Times and USA Today bestselling author of contemporary, paranormal, and young adult romance. Her works include the Montgomery Ink, Redwood Pack, Fractured Connections, and Elements of Five series, which have sold over 3.0 million books worldwide. She started writing while in graduate school for her advanced degree in chemistry and hasn't stopped since. Carrie Ann has written over seventy-five novels and novellas with more in the works. When she's not losing herself in her emotional and action-packed worlds, she's reading as much as she can while wrangling her clowder of cats who have more followers than she does.

www.CarrieAnnRyan.com